"Who is he?"

The familiar indigo eyes of the man in the picture were so vivid Noel could almost feel the black fire emanating from them. It was him! The man from her dream. The man whose touch had proven both soothing and arousing at the same time.

"Wolfe Longwalker. Whiskey River's most famous—or infamous—citizen. He was hanged as an outlaw." The shop owner answered Noel's question.

Into Noel's mind came the image of a single figure seated tall astride a horse, his hands tied behind his back, an ugly noose around his neck.

"He was also a writer," the woman continued, and pointed to some of Wolfe's books. Noel picked up several to buy, when another book caught her eye. *"Rogues Across Time."* She read the gold inlaid lettering out loud. When she turned a page and came face-to-face with Wolfe's glowering visage, she imagined she could feel the book growing warm in her hand.

"I'll buy it," she said. *And suddenly, very clearly, she saw Wolfe smiling at her....*

Dear Reader,

Over the years, I've received letters asking when I was going to write a book about Princess Noel, the youngest daughter in my Montacroix royal family. I always answer that I plan to do that, as soon as I find the right man for her.

When I first saw Wolfe Longwalker, seated astride a horse in the rain, with a rope around his neck, rigidly refusing to surrender to his captors, even at the moment of his hanging, I knew I'd finally found the man capable of teaching this intelligent woman, whom the paparazzi has dubbed The Ice Princess, the true meaning of passion.

In *The Outlaw*, I had the unique opportunity to return to the scene of my January MIRA title, *Confessions*. Set in the remote, rugged Arizona mountain area, this book kicks off my MEN OF WHISKEY RIVER series.

I envision Whiskey River as a romantic, magical place. A place where anything can happen. (And often does.) A town like Brigadoon, hidden in the mists, just waiting to be discovered.

I hope you enjoy Princess Noel's wild, out-of-time adventure in historical Whiskey River. I also hope you'll visit again, when the witch of Whiskey River starts brewing up trouble. And romance. The MEN OF WHISKEY RIVER return this fall.

Happy reading!

JoAnn Ross

I love hearing from readers. You can write to me at HC 31, Box 428, Happy Jack, AZ 86024, E-mail to JoAnnRoss@aol.com or visit on my Home Page on the World Wide Web at http://www.comet.net/writers/joann

JoAnn Ross
THE OUTLAW

Harlequin Books

TORONTO • NEW YORK • LONDON
AMSTERDAM • PARIS • SYDNEY • HAMBURG
STOCKHOLM • ATHENS • TOKYO • MILAN
MADRID • WARSAW • BUDAPEST • AUCKLAND

ISBN 0-373-25685-X

THE OUTLAW

Copyright © 1996 by JoAnn Ross.

Printed in U.S.A.

ROGUES

ROGUES ACROSS TIME

THE OUTLAW

The folklore of the Wild American West could not be complete without the outlaw. Portrayed as romantic heroes of the "wild, wild West" in dime novels and the *Police Gazette* (reportedly read by half the male population in America in the late nineteenth century), their violent exploits blaze on in the ballads and myths of a nation.

Wolfe Longwalker was the illegitimate son of an Irish-American cavalry officer and a Navajo mother who died after giving birth to him on the tribe's notorious forced walk to imprisonment at Fort Sumner. Wolfe eventually obtained revenge against his father's people. Not with bows and arrows, but with the formidable power of the white man's words. His stories of Indian life in the Arizona territory became worldwide bestsellers.

Despite his literary success, he was later convicted of murdering a family of white settlers—a crime dubbed "The Massacre at Whiskey River" by the *Gazette*—and sentenced to death by hanging. Before the sentence could be carried out, he escaped, eluding his captors for twelve days. But in the end, he was recaptured. And hanged.

Prologue

Arizona Territory, 1896

IT RAINED the day they hanged Wolfe Longwalker.

It was a cold spring afternoon, with an icy rain falling unceasingly from a darkened sky. Thunder boomed from anvil-shaped gunmyetal-gray clouds. The dirt road leading through Whiskey River had turned to thick mud—a red mire that smelled like horse dung and made a loud sucking sound as boots slogged through it.

Normally, such filthy weather would have kept the population of the isolated western town indoors drinking whiskey and brawling in the saloons or seeking pleasures of the flesh in the town's bordellos. But it wasn't every day a horse-stealing, murdering half-breed was going to be hanged.

Not even in Whiskey River.

The fact that Longwalker had been a thorn in the community's hide—or, as one drunken cowhand pointed out succinctly, another more vital anatomical part—made the day even more special.

The public hanging was being treated as a holiday. The bank and the general store were closed, as were the mines and sawmills, so workers could attend the hanging. Reporters for newspapers throughout the territory were on hand to record the event. The militia, having traveled from the territorial capital of Prescott, marched in precise formation through the muddy street.

The short, uneven expanse of warped and weathered boardwalk had been claimed by the women: ranchers' wives in bright, flower-sprigged calico skirts and starched white shirtwaists; farmers' and miners' wives in rough, pigeon-brown homespun; and prostitutes decked out in shiny, lace-trimmed satin and feathered hats all stood shoulder to shoulder in an atypically feminine unity.

"It's such a damn waste," one hennaed fallen dove complained. Crying openly, she blew her nose on a man's red-and-white bandanna.

Although no one answered, more than one so-called respectable female was seen surreptitiously dabbing her eyes with the corner of a lace-trimmed handkerchief.

The rain continued to fall.

The man responsible for the large turnout sat rigidly astride his blood bay mare, his hands tied behind his back. Wolfe Longwalker was wearing the same clothing he'd been wearing when captured two days earlier—buckskin trousers and a pair of bark-brown boots. His long jet hair was held back from his forehead with a red cotton headband. Rain ran in rivulets down a rigidly muscled chest the hue of burnished Arizona copper.

Normally, in bright sunlight, Wolfe's eyes were a dark blue, betraying his cavalryman father's Irish roots. On this overcast day, they appeared as black and hard as obsidian.

Appearing disinterested in the proceedings, Wolfe kept those dark eyes directed straight ahead as he looked out across the fierce red landscape where the Dineh—The People, *his* people—had once roamed with impunity.

A familiar cold anger flowed through his veins. As if sensing Wolfe's mood, the mare's nostrils flared, but she remained obediently still.

"Any last words?" a man sitting on a buckskin gelding asked.

Jess Buchanan, the territorial marshal who'd finally succeeded in tracking Wolfe down, was wearing a yellow oilskin slicker. Water streamed off the brim of his fawn Stetson, dripped from his thick handlebar mustache. Beneath the slicker, he was wearing a Colt .45 Peacemaker in a hand-tooled leather holster; in his hands he was holding a thick, braided rawhide rope.

Wolfe did not turn his gaze away from *Dook'o'oosliid*, one of the four mountains that marked the boundaries of the sacred Navajo earth.

"It is a waste of breath to talk to a coyote." He refused to look at his captor.

Despite the chill in the air, Buchanan's cheeks flushed a hot crimson, as if with fever. "Then you'd better start praying to the Great Spirit, Longwalker," he growled as he attempted to slip the heavy rope over Wolfe's dark head.

The mare snorted and nervously sidestepped. Cursing, the lawman tried again as the mostly drunk rabble began chanting its impatience with the delay.

"Quit jawin' and hang the murderin' Injun," one cowboy called out. He spit a long stream of Bull Durham juice into the mud.

"Send the son-of-a-bitch savage on his way to the happy hunting ground," a miner shouted. That suggestion received a burst of hearty laughter.

As the lawman managed to tug the noose tight, one woman wasn't laughing. "Don't you get any idea of droppin' by my place the next time you're in need of female comfort, Jess Buchanan," the redheaded whore yelled out. "Because the Road to Ruin is off limits to you from now on." Despite the raw emotionalism in Belle O'Roarke's voice, her threat only earned another round of male chuckles.

A drum rolled.

The uniformed troops drew their sabers and presented arms.

The marshal gave the rope an experimental tug. Satisfied that it would hold, he raised a black whip and slapped the mare's rump. Hard.

At the same time the whip struck the horse, a rolling clap of thunder boomed, echoing against the slate clouds like a hundred—a thousand—deerskin drums. A crack of lightning split the sky above the snow-covered sacred peak of *Dook'o'oosliid*. Whinnying her distress, Wolfe Longwalker's bay reared up on her hind legs. Then she took off running.

1

Montacroix, 1996

THE ALABASTER wedding-cake spires of the Giraudeau palace jutted through the silvery morning fog surrounding it, like Brigadoon rising from the mists. The scene, which had graced innumerable postcards, was familiar the world over. Set on an island in the middle of the sapphire waters of Lake Losange, the palace appeared both glamorous and serene at the same time.

But as so often was the case, appearances were deceiving. Inside the palace, the mood was anything but serene as staff and family bustled about, preparing for a royal wedding.

"Well? What do you think?"

Uncharacteristically on edge, Princess Noel Giraudeau de Montacroix surveyed her reflection in a gilt-framed mirror. The wedding gown was a floor-length tube of ivory satin; the refined sweetheart neckline and the long, pointed sleeves were adorned with white embroidery. A lace veil was held in place atop the princess's pale blond head by a pearl tiara.

Sabrina Giraudeau, Noel's sister-in-law and friend, chewed on a scarlet fingernail and treated the princess to a judicial look.

"I think it needs something," she said finally. "Some ruffles, maybe. A few flounces. At least a decent train."

Noel laughed. "I should have known better than to ask for fashion advice from a woman who got married in a hoopskirt."

"Hey, it worked for Scarlett O'Hara. Besides, Burke liked it." An attractive color rose in Sabrina's cheeks as she recalled exactly how much her husband had also enjoyed taking the voluminous dress off her once they were alone after the day-long celebration of their public nuptials.

"Really, Noel," she said, returning to the discussion at hand, "your usual conservative style is fine for the office. But hopefully, a woman gets married only once in her life. You should pull out all the stops. Like I did."

Indeed, Sabrina Darling's marriage could have come from the pages of a fairy tale. It had all the proper ingredients—a dashing prince charming, a beautiful, but impoverished bride and enough glitz and glamour to have people still talking more than three years later.

"Burke is regent," Noel said. "Your son will rule Montacroix some day. I'm merely the youngest Giraudeau daughter."

"You're still a princess," Sabrina argued. "And you owe it to the people of Montacroix to show up at your wedding dressed like one."

"That's unfair," Noel protested laughingly.

Everyone in the family knew Noel's deep-seated sense of royal obligation. All her life, the princess had tried to live up to other's expectations. She'd dedicated herself to the tenets of duty and loyalty to her family. And country.

While her older sister, Chantal, had been jet-setting all over the world, Noel had been in school in London and Paris and Geneva, earning degrees in business and public policy.

While her half brother, Prince Burke, had been heading up the Montacroix polo team, winning Grand Prix races and being voted the most eligible bachelor in the western world, Noel had labored as head of her country's social services agency, struggling to find ways to maintain Montacroix's generosity to its citizens while remaining competitive in a global business climate.

It was not that she didn't enjoy her work, because she did. And it wasn't that she envied Chantal or Burke. The truth was, Noel had always been more than happy to leave the spotlight to her two more famous siblings.

The only reserved member of one of the world's most glamorous families, there were times when Noel almost felt like a changeling, left on the palace's marble doorstep by mistake.

"You need more oomph," Sabrina pressed her case.

"Oomph?" Although her native language was French, Noel's English, thanks in part to her American mother, was impeccable. She normally had no trouble with idioms, but this term was unfamiliar.

"Pizzazz. You know, pow!"

"Ah." Noel nodded. "Pizzazz."

Noel decided that single word described Sabrina to a tee. Dressed in a crimson cashmere sweater, matching leggings and fringed red leather boots, the former Broadway actress reminded her of Will Scarlet.

"I'm not suggesting that you wear thirty pounds of beading and crinolines like I did, Noel, honey." Sabrina's voice carried a honied south-of-the-Mason-Dixon-line accent. "But you really should jazz up that dress just a little."

She grinned, then played her trump card. "Just think of Bertran's face when you walk down the aisle looking like something out of *Sleeping Beauty*."

The idea was enough to make Noel smile. "He wouldn't recognize me."

Noel's fiancé, Bertran Rostand, was vice president of the Montacroix Bank. He was also a very distant cousin. And her best friend.

Stifling a slight sigh, Noel continued to study her reflection in the gilt-framed mirror and did her best to ignore the vague misgivings about her dress and her upcoming marriage.

Displaying a tenacity that had always served her well, Sabrina was not ready to give up. "You know Chantal would agree with me."

"Probably. But my sister and I are different."

Now, *that*, Noel considered, was definitely an understatement. Once described by a particularly ebullient society columnist as the quintessential fairy-tale princess, Chantal's jet-set existence had brought her fame and scandal prior to her marriage.

These past years, however, the ultraglamorous princess who'd once kept an entire army of paparazzi working overtime to keep up with her, was happily settled down with her husband and two children in Washington, D.C. Caine O'Bannion, Chantal's husband, a former Secret Service agent, operated a private security firm, while Chantal continued to gain acclaim as a gifted artist.

"Oh, that reminds me," Sabrina said, reaching into a pocket of her sweater, "you received a letter from Chantal today. Your mother asked me to bring it up to you."

Grateful for an excuse to move the subject away from her admittedly restrained wedding gown, Noel opened the cream envelope. "It's an invitation. To her latest fund-raiser."

Along with her painting, Chantal had continued her fund-raising efforts for her beloved Rescue the Children foundation. It had been on such a tour to the United States that Chantal had met the handsome American hero who would become her husband.

"She's sponsoring a gallery showing of unknown western artists." Noel skimmed the invitation. "The week after my wedding."

"It's too bad you're going to be on your honeymoon," Sabrina said, knowing of Noel's fascination with the American West.

"The timing could certainly be better." Noel wished she could get more excited about the planned cruise through the Greek Isles.

For the cover of the engraved invitation, Chantal had selected a woodcut sketch depicting a group of Indians on horseback watching a settler's log cabin burn. The title read: Massacre at Whiskey River. As she studied the drawing in more detail, although it made no sense at all, Noel could hear drunken laughter, the faint sound of a piano, the clatter of poker chips. She could smell cigar smoke and beer and whiskey. And overly sweet perfume.

"Noel?"

Noel belatedly realized that Sabrina had been talking to her. "I'm sorry." Slightly disoriented, she shook her head in an attempt to clear it.

"Are you all right?"

The prudent thing to do was to lie. Noel opened her mouth to assure her sister-in-law that she was fine, when an image shimmered in her mind's eye. A misty picture of a single figure, seated tall astride a horse, his hands tied behind his back. Her fingers tightened on the edges of the engraved invitation.

"No." Noel barely recognized her own faint, shaky voice. "Sabrina, something's very, very wrong."

"Not with the dress."

It was not a question. Just last month, Noel had told Sabrina and Burke that their dream of parenthood would soon be realized. Two days later, they'd received a telephone call from their attorney, informing them that an infant boy had just been born in a Montacroix hospital. A child whose young, unmarried mother was making the ultimate maternal sacrifice in putting him up for adoption.

If she'd harbored any doubts about Noel having allegedly inherited the gift of second sight from her Gypsy grandmother, that day Sabrina had definitely become a believer.

"No. It's not the dress."

Noel began to shiver, suddenly overwhelmed by the feeling of a cold rain that chilled all the way to the bone. But the rain was not as icy as a vivid, visual picture of a man's remarkably blue, angry eyes.

"Excuse me, Sabrina, but I have to telephone Chantal."

BEFORE THE DAY had ended, Noel was on her way to the Montacroix airport, where she was booked on a flight to Paris. From there, she'd take an Air France Concorde flight to New York, then change to American

Airlines for another flight to Phoenix, where she'd arranged to rent a car to drive to Whiskey River, Arizona. The remote ranching community was located in the northern mountains near the Navajo Indian reservation.

"I still do not understand why you have to leave now," her father, Prince Eduard, complained gruffly. Puzzled by her uncharacteristically rash behavior, her parents had insisted on accompanying her to the airport.

"I don't exactly understand, myself," Noel admitted. "All I know is that I don't have any choice. I have some important connection with this sketch, Papa, I feel it. Since Chantal tells me the sketch is from Arizona, I must go there."

"That sketch," Eduard told her, "is a hundred years old. And even with your gift—"

"Eduard, dear." Jessica Giraudeau placed a calming hand atop her husband's. "We must allow Noel to follow her feelings," she counseled. "As Burke and Chantal have done."

She gifted him with the soft, coaxing smile that had once charmed legions of men who'd sat in darkened theaters all over the world, dreaming impossible dreams as they watched the actress on the silver screen. Any man who'd ever met the ultraglamorous Jessica Thorne had wanted her. But Prince Eduard Giraudeau de Montacroix had been the one to win her hand. As well as her heart.

"As we did," Jessica said, reminding him of their own rocky courtship. A courtship that had nearly cost the prince his crown.

Eduard was not easily deterred. "Even if it destroys her chance for happiness?" Both women understood that his frustration was an attempt to mask his fatherly concern. "What if you do not return in time for the ceremony? Do you think Bertran is going to wait forever?"

Noel refrained from pointing out that her fiancé had already patiently waited years, ever since first proposing to her on her seventeenth birthday. Such unwavering affection was admirable in these days of short-term relationships, she reminded herself.

"It's a moot point, Papa," Noel murmured.

The truth was that lately she'd been having strange, disloyal feelings about Bertran, feelings that she could not put into words. Why was it that her upcoming nuptials were causing her more misgivings than whatever might be awaiting her in Arizona?

"Because I'll be back in time for you to walk me down the aisle."

"I am pleased to hear that." He nodded his satisfaction as he turned the Rolls-Royce onto the road leading to the terminal. "Because your mother worries."

ALTHOUGH THE Air France flight attendants unfailingly upheld the airline's tradition of *esprit de service*, Noel grew increasingly on edge as the plane sped across the sky on its way to America.

After picking unenthusiastically at what she knew was undoubtedly a superb meal of grilled squab and tender roasted potatoes, she turned on her overhead light and attempted to settle down with a copy of the *London Financial Journal*. But the text could have been written in Sanskrit, for all the sense it made to her.

Sighing, she turned instead to this month's issue of French *Elle*, but the magazine failed to capture her attention. Instead, her mind kept rerunning the rainy scene of the man on horseback. Who was he? And why was he calling out to her?

Finally, sheer exhaustion got the better of her. Noel leaned her head back against the gray leather seat, closed her eyes and instantly fell into a deep, almost trancelike sleep and began to dream.

There was music—someone, somewhere, was playing the piano. Her body ached. Uncomfortable, she shifted on the satin sheets beneath her.

"The girl's in pretty bad shape," she heard a female voice say. The sweet scent of lilacs and roses drifted closer, mingling with the pleasant aroma of juniper wood emanating from a nearby fireplace.

"Her injuries appear worse than they are." The man's voice was as deep and dark as a starless night.

"That's a good thing," the woman responded. "Since the poor little thing looks like something the cat dragged in."

The man mumbled something Noel could not quite catch. Then, "Hand me that bowl."

A moment later, she felt a cool cloth stroking her throbbing forehead and breathed in the soothing scent of lavender water. The cloth moved over her face, down her neck, across her shoulder blades. When he hit a tender spot, she flinched and moaned again.

"Shh." He pressed a fingertip against her lip, then brushed her hair back from her forehead with an infinitely tender touch.

She was basking in the comforting touch, when the voice of the flight attendant, announcing their immi-

nent arrival in New York, caused the dream to shatter
into a thousand crystalline pieces.

Still unsettled from the vivid, too-real dream, Noel
managed to thank the smiling young woman for the
warm moist towel the attendants always handed out
prior to landing. As she washed her face and hands,
Noel imagined that the white cloth carried the soothing scent of lavender.

2

Whiskey River, 1896

THE DREAM CREPT into Wolfe Longwalker's mind shortly before dawn, his thoughts tangling with a woman who was dreaming of him. Her hair was as pale as corn silk bathed in the golden glow of July sunshine. Her scent, as fragrant as a meadow in full bloom, surrounded him, infiltrating his mind, tantalizing his senses. Unable to resist the creamy lure of her skin, he reached out and touched her cheek with his fingertips, finding it to be just as soft as he'd imagined.

He drew her into his arms, but as he lowered his mouth to her softly smiling one, she vanished, like the seductive dream she was.

Cursing, Wolfe pushed himself off the wood-plank floor where he'd been sleeping, having found the cot too short and too narrow. He walked to the barred window and looked out at the wooden scaffold that was being built in his honor.

As he planned his escape, the dream, and the woman, faded from his mind.

Whiskey River, 1996

THIRTY-SIX LONG and exhausting hours after leaving Montacroix, Noel was in love. She had, of course, traveled to her mother's home country many times. But except for an occasional trip to southern California, she'd never been west of Chicago. Until now.

All her life she'd been enamored with the mythology of the American Southwest, fostered by countless movies. But never had she expected the reality of the landscape—the wild, cactus-studded Sonoran desert, the towering red sandstone rocks, endless blue sky and constantly changing, dramatic light—to transcend the larger-than-life myth.

Arizona was bigger than she'd thought it would be, and far more beautiful than its depiction in any movie.

It was, she decided, one of the rare instances in life when the actual did not destroy the validity of the imagined. For a woman who'd grown up in a small landlocked Alpine country, the vastness of this panoramic pastel land, rolling away in all directions, empty of everything but beauty, quite literally took her breath away.

According to the travel guide she'd bought in the Phoenix Sky Harbor terminal, Whiskey River was home to three hundred and fifty full-time residents and at least triple that many during the summer, when vacationers came streaming north to escape the desert heat. Noel felt an instant flash of recognition as she drove down the main street. Which wasn't all that surprising, she decided, since her book had also informed her that the town had served as a movie set on more than one occasion. Gene Autry, John Wayne and Clint Eastwood had all ridden horseback down Main Street. So had Doc Holliday and Wyatt Earp.

She also knew the man in her dream had been here, as well.

Her ever-efficient secretary had booked her into a bed and breakfast a few miles outside Whiskey River that had, until recently, been a working ranch.

As she checked into the inn, the owner, Audrey Bradshaw, a pleasingly plump woman in her mid-sixties, explained to Noel that the cattle had been sold off last year.

"Now that Jake's gone," Audrey revealed, "I've just about decided to move to one of those retirement communities in Phoenix or Tucson. It gets too lonely out here."

"I can see how it might feel that way," Noel murmured politely, wondering how anyone could bear to leave such a heavenly spot.

"Not that it wouldn't be a real good deal," Audrey said. Dressed in period clothing, the woman was wearing a white apron over a blue, flower-sprigged calico dress. Her unnaturally strawberry-red hair had been permed into wild corkscrew curls that would suit someone far younger than her age. "For the right person. Jake and I were real happy here for more than forty years. Had all my kids in the same hand-carved bed upstairs that Jake was born in."

Noel, more than most people, could understand roots. "I was born at home, too."

"Well, isn't that nice." Audrey nodded her head, causing the red curls to bob like springs. "Not many young folks can say that." She handed Noel an old-fashioned brass key. "Be sure to check out the museum."

"Museum?"

"Through there." She nodded in the direction of a red velvet curtain.

Noel had always believed that there were two types of travelers. Those who were willing to live haphazardly out of suitcases and those who, immediately upon arrival at their destination, could not relax until they'd unpacked.

She had always been one of the latter.

But today, some inner instinct drew her through the draperies.

Restored with what appeared to be genuine antiques, the room, which smelled of lemon oil and vanilla potpourri, boasted a high ceiling with thick crown molding, sponged burgundy walls and brass wall sconces. Garlands of red and pink roses and dark green leaves spread lushly across the ivory carpet.

"Welcome to the Road to Ruin's rogues' gallery," Audrey said as she joined Noel.

"The Road to Ruin?" Noel asked absently, her gaze drawn to a life-size cardboard cutout of a man standing in the corner of the room.

"This place used to be a brothel. Back in the olden days."

"How fascinating." Noel smiled, tempted to call her overprotective father and tell him she was staying in a Wild West brothel.

She crossed the carpet and stood looking up into a pair of familiar indigo eyes, so vivid she could almost feel the black fire emanating from them. A cold chill ran up her spine, in direct contrast to the fingers of heat uncurling in her belly.

It was him! The man from her dream. The man whose touch had proven both soothing and arousing at the same time. She could hear his voice, brushing like ebony velvet against all her nerve endings. Suddenly, she was hit by a strong rush of emotion. So strong that Noel had to remind herself to breathe.

"Who is this?" Her voice, displaying her sudden emotional turmoil, was not as confident as usual.

Although she still had no idea why she'd been so irresistibly drawn to Arizona, Noel knew, with every fiber of her being, that it had everything to do with this man.

"That's Wolfe Longwalker. Whiskey River's most famous—or infamous, depending on your point of view—citizen." Audrey grinned. "He's a sexy son of a gun, isn't he?"

"He's quite—" Noel paused, seeking the right word "—striking." She sensed, with the inborn intuition she'd learned to trust, that this was a man who'd known a great deal of tragedy.

Depicted by the artist as clad solely in boots and a pair of fawn-hued buckskin trousers, Wolfe Longwalker wasn't conventionally handsome, but he was undeniably sensual.

His cheekbones were a sharp slash riding high on his lean dark face; his hair, as black as ebony and as straight as rainwater, hung to his shoulders. His lips were set in a straight grim line that revealed not an ounce of softness.

Although his dark blue-black eyes were truly riveting, and made the hairs at her nape tingle, Noel managed to pull her gaze away and make a judicious study of the rest of the man. Commanding muscles rippled in his arms and shoulders, across his chest and down his flat, rigid stomach.

"It's a remarkably lifelike image," she murmured, feeling a foolish urge to reach out and touch the cardboard, to see if that tawny copper flesh was as warm as it looked. "Did you paint it?"

"Oh, no. It was done by some graphics company in southern California. They created it on a computer from an old tintype. We figured the inn needed its own outlaw. What with all its colorful history and all."

"He was an outlaw?" That didn't feel at all right.

"Well, to tell you the truth, the jury's still out on that one," Audrey allowed, crossing her arms over her abundant chest. "But he sure as hell was hanged as one."

"Hanged." The image returned to shimmer in her mind's eye. That unnerving, misty picture of a single figure she now knew to be Wolfe Longwalker, seated tall astride a horse, his hands tied behind his back. The image shifted into focus long enough for her to view the ugly noose around his neck.

"In town," she murmured. "In the street."

"Yep." Audrey nodded. "The original scaffold got hit by lightning and burned down before the hanging. What with all the threats of an Indian uprising, the marshal didn't want to take time to build a new one." She eyed Noel with renewed interest. "If you knew about that, I guess you must have heard of him."

The room was closing in around her. Noel had to resist rubbing her arms to warm her suddenly cold skin. "Not really."

"Perhaps you've seen a picture. There was a sketch artist did a drawing for the Denver paper after Wolfe was hanged. It showed up in a *National Geographic* issue about the Wild West a few years ago."

"Yes. I've seen a picture." Noel took a steadying breath and did not elaborate.

"Well, we've got a lot of those," the woman said with a wave of her hand, directing Noel to the photos hung in wooden frames on the burgundy wall. "Too bad there weren't any photographs taken of Wolfe the day of the hanging."

"What was he accused of doing?"

"Some German settlers outside of town—mom, dad, three kids—were shot by Indians and their cabin burned to the ground. Evidence pointed right at Wolfe bein' the ringleader.

"Though people around these parts still argue to this day whether Wolfe was really the killer. Or just a rabble-rouser who managed to stick like a burr beneath the saddles of most of the ranchers in the territory." Audrey handed her a faded sepia photograph. "I suppose one of the reasons folks were willin' to think the worst of Wolfe was the fact that he didn't exactly hang out with the pillars of the community."

Noel studied the photograph depicting two men and a woman. One was obviously Wolfe Longwalker, looking incredibly handsome in a dark suit. With him was another man dressed in a similar suit and holding a top hat in his right hand. Standing between them, clad in the style of the late 1800s, was a striking brunette woman.

"She's beautiful," Noel murmured. "But her eyes are so sad."

"Maybe she had an inkling how things were going to turn out in the end," Audrey suggested. "That's Etta Place and Harry Longabaugh. The Sundance Kid," she elaborated at Noel's blank look. "Before Sundance and Butch Cassidy went off and supposedly got themselves killed in Bolivia."

"I've seen the movie." Indeed, in her younger years, she'd had a secret crush on Robert Redford. "I like to believe they escaped."

"Me, too," Audrey agreed. "There was talk that Etta and Wolfe supposedly had a little something goin' on the side—Wolfe was supposed to be one helluva ladies' man. But I've always figured that his affair with Etta was just rumor.

"Wolfe may have been a pain in the ass, and there's an outside chance that he might even have been a murderer. But the guy was too smart to make the mistake of creeping into Etta's tepee. Harry would've shot him dead right on the spot."

Murmuring something that could have been agreement, Noel picked up a slender paperback novel. "*First Man, First Woman.* By Wolfe Longwalker?"

Audrey nodded. "Wolfe wrote a lot of books. He was kind of the Zane Grey of Indians."

Noel studied another entitled *The Night Way.* "I've never heard of him."

"Not many people have. Probably because he was an Indian. But I guess he was real popular in his time. Back East, that is. Out here, his version of how the West was won hit a little too close to home.

"The books went out of print ages ago. The Navajo Tribal Council reprinted some of them. They just came out last week and they're already selling like hotcakes."

Noel took the hint. Not that she needed any prompting where Wolfe Longwalker was concerned. "I'll buy them." She added a volume entitled *Sand Paintings on A Hogan Floor and Other Short Stories* to the others. "This one, too."

"Good choice. That's my favorite of the three." While Audrey rang up the sale, Noel roamed the room and continued to study the old photos and newspaper clippings depicting Whiskey River's rambunctious past, and most particularly, the turbulent life and times of Wolfe Longwalker.

She was just about to return to the old-fashioned cash register, when another book caught her eye. *"Rogues Across Time?"* she read the gold inlaid lettering out loud.

"What's that?" Audrey's forehead furrowed in a puzzled frown.

Noel picked up the weathered text and began leafing through the pages. "It appears to be a collection of short stories about various adventurers." Each story was accompanied by a black-and-white ink drawing.

"I don't remember buying that." The innkeeper's frown deepened. "Who's the author?"

"I don't know." Noel held up the brown book for Audrey's perusal. "There's some type of stain over the name."

"Oh, well," Audrey decided with a shrug, "my memory isn't what it used to be, that's for sure. I must have gotten it in that barrel of old westerns Newt Wattson sold me when he needed money to pay off his drunk-and-disorderly fine."

It *definitely* was a rogues' gallery, Noel determined as she leafed through the stories of pirates and highwaymen and gunslingers. When she turned a page and came face-to-face with Wolfe's glowering visage, she imagined she could feel the book growing warm in her hands.

"I'll buy it." She placed the book on the counter.

Audrey examined it for a price sticker. "It's pretty weather-beaten. How about two bucks?"

"Two dollars seems more than fair." Noel did not volunteer that she would have been willing to pay a hundred times that.

"It's hard to imagine a man with so much going for him, professionally, killing a family of innocent people for no apparent reason," Noel murmured, more to herself than to her gregarious hostess.

Perhaps this was what she was doing here in Whiskey River, she considered, trying to make sense out of a situation that defied logic. Perhaps she was here to clear Wolfe Longwalker's name.

"I always thought that was kinda odd, too." Audrey shrugged her well-padded shoulders once again. "But, those settlers were sure as shootin' dead. And someone had to have done it. I guess we'll never know for certain what happened at that cabin out at Whiskey River. "Besides," she said, an irrepressible dimple creasing her powdered cheek, "if Wolfe hadn't become an outlaw, people probably wouldn't want to have their picture taken with him."

"Have their picture taken?"

"I can make a sepia print of you standing beside the cutout. Five bucks a picture. Three poses for ten dollars. And that includes a period costume and a cardboard folder with an easel back." She handed Noel her change. "Makes a real nice souvenir."

Noel turned back to the life-size cardboard figure. Although she suspected she was letting her imagination run away with her, she could almost read the mocking challenge in those indigo eyes.

"Perhaps another time," she said, shaking off the strange feeling. "I'm a little tired."

"Well, of course you are," Audrey clucked sympathetically. "After your long trip. What you need now is a nice hot bubble bath, a glass of wine and a good night's sleep. Perhaps you'd like to pose with Wolfe tomorrow."

Noel dragged her gaze from the figure of Wolfe Longwalker and gathered up her purchases. "Perhaps."

"I'll bring the wine right up."

"If you don't mind, I think I'll forgo the wine." Noel offered her most charming smile. "Jet lag." A frequent traveler, she'd never suffered jet lag in her life.

Audrey seemed determined to prove herself a good hostess. "Tea then," she suggested. "I've some nice herbal tea that should hit the spot."

Someone, somewhere in time, was belting out a chorus of "The Yellow Rose of Texas" on the piano. Once again, Noel heard the sound of laughter. The clink of glasses. She pressed the fingers of her right hand against her temple and took a deep breath.

Royal training, drilled into her from the cradle, proved invaluable as Noel managed a smile. "Herbal tea sounds wonderful."

After a soothing soak in the lion-footed bathtub and nearly an entire pot of Audrey's steaming-hot Red Zinger tea—which the animated innkeeper had served with a plate of rich dark homemade brownies—Noel's normally rocklike equilibrium had returned.

Enough so that she forced herself to unpack before turning to the book of short stories that were calling to her like a siren song.

As she took the clothing from her luggage, Noel's mind wandered, as it did so often these days, to her fiancé.

She loved Bertran. Truly.

She extracted a long silk nightgown from its folds of snowy tissue paper and placed it in the top drawer of the dresser.

Unfortunately, she considered as she returned to the suitcase for panties and bras, there were times, and this was one of them, when it crossed her mind that looking at her childhood playmate was like looking in the mirror.

They were both studious, intensely serious-minded individuals. Both could also be accused of being workaholics. Noel couldn't remember the last time Bertran had done anything just for fun.

"And you're just as bad," she muttered.

A picture of the two of them, sitting side by side in a lacy, flower-bedecked wedding bed, talking on their individual cellular phones while engrossed in their individual schedules and timetables and stacks of dry data flickered unattractively through her mind.

"You love him," she reminded herself firmly. "And he loves you."

So why, she asked herself with growing frustration, did her upcoming marriage to the handsome Montacroix banker—which had come as a surprise to absolutely no one in the kingdom—make her feel so despondent?

She shook her head in self-disgust as she took a trio of cashmere sweaters and matching slacks from the suitcase.

"What's the good of inheriting Katia's gift," she asked herself, "if it can't work for me?"

Experience had taught Noel that when it came to her own life, she was no more psychic than the next woman. As she stacked the sweaters on the shelf of an antique pine armoire, she decided she was going to have to come to terms with her misgivings. And soon. Because once she walked down the aisle of the historic Montacroix Cathedral and pledged her troth to Bertran, she would be Madame Rostand for life.

"I love him," she insisted, closing the armoire door with more force than necessary. "I do!"

More than a little frustrated, she poured out the last of the tea and climbed into the high four-poster bed with *Rogues Across Time* and turned to the section on Wolfe Longwalker.

Wolfe was the illegitimate son of a U.S. Cavalry officer who'd been in charge of guarding the women captured during Kit Carson's campaign against the Navajo during their internment at Fort Defiance. Whiskey River's most infamous citizen had been born during the tribe's notorious three-hundred-mile forced "Long Walk" to imprisonment at Fort Sumner. Hence his last name. His first name, Noel read, was due to a birthmark in the shape of a wolf's head, on the inside of his wrist.

His weak, exhausted, half-starved mother had died after giving birth along the trail, which gave Wolfe every reason to hate his father's people. According to the unknown author, he'd spent his early years plotting revenge.

Which he eventually obtained. Not with bows and arrows or the ubiquitous Winchester rifle, but with the formidable power of the white man's words. After returning from the missionary school the government Indian agency had sent him to back East, he'd been apprenticed to a Whiskey River newspaperman. It was there Wolfe had learned that the pen truly was mightier than the sword.

His reports of Indian life in the Arizona Territory had proven immensely popular with those same Easterners who'd made Frederic Remington a household name. His stories were printed in the *Atlantic Monthly, Harper's Weekly* and the *New York Herald.* His books became bestsellers not only in the United States, but in Europe, as well, earning him an audience with Queen Victoria. The elderly monarch, Noel read, had appeared suitably charmed by the powerful, handsome young man.

Intrigued, Noel turned next to Wolfe Longwalker's book of short stories.

The tea had gone cold, but totally immersed in the starkly drawn, yet mesmerizing depiction of Wolfe Longwalker's long-ago Navajo world, Noel didn't notice.

It was late when she finished reading. Although she was exhausted, Noel couldn't fall asleep.

She spent the long night lying in the cozy four-poster bed, staring out the window at the seemingly endless expanse of starlit sky, thinking about Bertran. And her upcoming marriage.

But most of all, Noel thought about Wolfe Longwalker.

3

WHEN SHE CAME downstairs the following morning, Noel discovered that Audrey took the breakfast part of her bed-and-breakfast commitment very seriously.

"Breakfast was Jake's favorite meal," Audrey confided as she poured Noel a cup of steaming coffee. "It's a pleasure to have people to cook for again."

Not wanting to throw cold water on Audrey's obvious enjoyment, Noel did her best to make inroads on the amazing variety of fruit and muffins, but turned down her hostess's offer of a western omelet, Canadian bacon and hash-brown potatoes.

While she ate, she opened the copy of *Rogues Across Time* she'd brought downstairs with her, rereading the part about Wolfe's alleged crime.

The author obviously believed the Indian writer had not committed the murders that resulted in his hanging. But believing and proving were two different things. Especially since there was no proof that anyone other than Wolfe Longwalker had killed those settlers.

Since his jury consisted solely of local ranchers, it came as no surprise to anyone when he was convicted of the cold-blooded massacre of five settlers—three of them under the age of eight. The other men, who had presumably returned to the reservation, were never sought. Apparently, capturing the alleged ringleader satisfied everyone's blood lust for revenge.

"The Massacre at Whiskey River," Noel murmured. Reaching into the pocket of her suede and denim jacket, she pulled out Chantal's invitation and studied the woodcut depicting the event.

Considering that this was yet more proof that she'd been drawn here to clear Wolfe Longwalker's name, she returned the engraved invitation to her pocket and continued reading.

The territorial judge had sentenced Wolfe to death by hanging, but before the sentence could be carried out, Noel read, he'd escaped. He'd managed to elude his captors for twelve days, but in the end, he'd been recaptured. And hanged.

Noel closed the book with a sigh and rubbed her temples. During her sleepless night, she'd come to the conclusion that she'd been brought to Whiskey River to clear Wolfe's name. She'd also decided the best way to start her quest was to see where Wolfe's life had ended.

After thanking Audrey for the breakfast, she left the inn, headed toward Whiskey River in her rental car. The rain, which had been a soft drizzle when she'd awakened, turned into a downpour. It was as if the sky had opened up overhead: thunder rumbled, lightning flashed and torrential rainfall lashed against the windshield, rendering the wipers nearly useless.

Her fingers tightened on the steering wheel as she leaned forward and tried, with scant success, to see the road. She supposed the water was much-needed in this arid land, but it certainly made driving on the slick narrow road a challenge, even for someone who'd grown up in the Alps.

The radio, tuned to a Winslow country station, began to crackle with static, stretching Noel's already taut nerves even tighter. She reached out and pushed the scan button.

She'd only taken her eyes from the road for an instant. But it was long enough. When she looked up again, she saw a horse and rider galloping straight toward her.

She twisted the wheel. Hard. The brakes locked up, throwing the rental car into a wild skid which she desperately tried to control, but couldn't.

The car rolled over, coming to a shuddering stop on its crushed roof. The bloodred mare, which had just barely avoided being struck, whinnied loudly. The car horn blared.

And then there was only deadly silence.

And the lonely sound of falling rain.

1896

IT WAS NOT GOING to be easy, Wolfe told himself as he galloped through the rain, away from Whiskey River. Certainly not as easy as escaping from that ramshackle wood and stone building the marshal laughingly called a jail. Or retrieving his mare from the terrified stable hand at the livery.

He knew that as soon as they discovered him missing, they'd be after him. He also knew that there'd be a hefty price on his head. He was, after all, a very convenient scapegoat.

His trial had been nothing more than a kangaroo court. A parade of witnesses had taken the stand, each placing his hand on the Bible, before swearing to some aspect of the Indian's guilt.

That they were lying under oath had not seemed to bother them. He suspected they'd been paid to put aside any fears of divine retribution. Such behavior didn't surprise him; he'd already discovered that white men were willing to do just about anything for money.

Which was what those killings were all about.

The Anglo ranchers, who conspired to steal land that had once belonged to his people in order to graze their cattle, had all the forces of the United States government behind them. With guns and laws, they succeeded in having the Dineh rounded up and consigned to a small corner of the world Wolfe's mother's people had originally claimed.

Not so long ago, the Navajo had roamed the land as far as the eye could see. Now there were houses. And towns, like Whiskey River. And all because the white man had discovered precious metals and coal in the distant, purple-hazed mountains.

The whites wanted the mountain timber for their houses, and the grassland, home to the elk and the deer, for grazing their cattle. That it belonged to Indians did not sit well with these white newcomers. These men who made their fortunes at the expense of others.

And now, the very same ranchers who'd stolen the Dineh's land were being vexed by a new group of settlers. Families who'd come West, foolishly believing that they could farm this arid, high desert rangeland. They were determined to conquer the land; diverting streams, pumping the water with their windmills, and with their sharp plows, ripping open the earth until she bled. The final straw had come when they'd begun stringing barbed wire over what had been open range.

That such intruders had to go had been obvious to the ranchers. It was, admittedly, preferable that they leave willingly. But those who stubbornly dug in their heels were treated by the ranchers to harsher methods.

And if the Indians could be blamed, so much the better.

Everyone knew what was happening. Wolfe suspected that there were even those white men who considered murder for profit wrong. Unfortunately, they hadn't been on his jury.

He didn't have a plan. There was, of course, always Mexico, although that was too obvious for his liking. Another possibility was to make to California, where he could become lost in the mining camps and goldfields of the Sierra Madre.

He could go to Alaska, that place where some old-time medicine men professed his people had once lived. Or to New York, where he had powerful friends in the publishing world who'd help him attain honest legal counsel, rather than the drunken, half-wit who'd been assigned his case by the territorial governor. The lawyer had been recommended to the governor by a coalition of Whiskey River ranchers who had their own reasons for wanting Wolfe Longwalker to hang. His stories depicting native life, which had so caught on back East where the laws were made, did nothing to further the ranchers' cause.

He was not without choices, Wolfe reminded himself as he galloped his mare, hell-bent for leather, away from Whiskey River. The thing to do was to get to the reservation where he could hide out in the canyons until he decided which option was best.

The rain was pouring from the blackened sky, making visibility difficult. But he was a man of the land, accustomed to such powerful Father rains.

Wolfe would later decide that it was his inattentiveness that caused him to ride into the path of that black buggy.

His mare saw it at the same time he did. Wolfe pulled up hard on the reins at the instant the mare rose back on her hind legs. Only the immense power in his inner thighs kept him from being flung headfirst over the horse's head.

Unfortunately, the driver of the buggy was not so lucky. Its horse reared, as well, causing the carriage to overturn. The horse broke free of its harness and tore off into the rain.

Cursing, Wolfe dismounted and walked over to the woman who'd been thrown free.

She'd landed beneath a tree, on a thick layer of pine needles that had fortuitously cushioned the blow. When he rolled her over, a faint sense of recognition tugged, but concerned by her unconscious state, Wolfe didn't stop to dwell on it. Kneeling beside her, he bent down and felt the soft breath coming from her pale lips. He picked up her wrist to check her pulse. Her blood-beat was thready, but even.

A knot was rising on her forehead, which explained her unconsciousness. He combed his fingers through her wet hair, looking for scalp wounds and finding none. Turning his attention to the rest of her, he ran his hands first down her arms, then her legs. When his probing touch drew a response, he took her ragged moan as a good sign and unbuttoned her denim and suede jacket.

Beneath the jacket she was wearing a silk shirt. It crossed his mind that the combination of rough denim and silk was an intriguing, if unorthodox, choice. It also made it more difficult to pinpoint exactly who—and what—she was.

Most of the women who wore denim in territorial Arizona were miners' wives, who labored long hard days working hardscrabble claims alongside their husbands.

Silk was reserved for whores and the occasional cavalry commander's wife who quickly learned that the fabric was highly impractical in a place where, too often, the laundry was beaten to near death in huge copper kettles over a fire.

The fact that this woman was not wearing a wedding band suggested she was no officer's wife. And her complexion was too smooth, her skin too soft, her scent too subtle for a whore.

Her blouse was fastened with tiny pearl buttons that echoed the pearls adorning her earlobes. Having traveled among the royalty of Europe, Wolfe recognized the pearl earrings to be of excellent quality. Nearly as excellent as the icy diamond she was wearing on the fourth finger of her left hand.

Whoever this woman was, she was obviously wealthy. Which meant, Wolfe determined grimly, that when she didn't arrive wherever she'd been headed, people would undoubtedly begin searching for her.

Frustration laced with impatience roughened his touch as he continued to probe for injuries. When his fingers pressed against a rib, she flinched. When they moved down her side, she moaned.

But still her eyes did not open.

Assuring himself that his interest was solely that of the Good Samaritan, Wolfe unbuttoned her silk blouse. Rocking back on his heels, he gazed in surprise at the skimpy band of flowered lace that barely covered her breasts in lieu of a more proper camisole.

Her torso was bare. Her flesh was as smooth as her silk blouse and distractingly fragrant. From what he could tell, her ribs were not broken, but merely bruised.

When his fingers brushed against the sides of her breasts, her lids flew open and he found himself suddenly staring down into a pair of eyes that were as crystal blue as the lakes in the territory's high country.

Again a faint memory stirred in the far reaches of his mind, one Wolfe could not quite grasp.

She stared in disbelief at the man glaring down at her. "I don't understand—"

"Your buggy ran in front of my horse." Wolfe knew he sounded overly defensive, but didn't apologize. "It overturned and you were thrown out."

"My buggy." Noel thought about that for a moment and decided this had to be another dream. "And you're Wolfe Longwalker."

"You've got the wrong man," he lied gruffly.

"No." She studied him, her solemn gaze moving slowly over his face. "It's you."

"What do you want with Longwalker?"

"I want to help him."

It was his turn to study her. She appeared to be telling the truth. But there was still the unpalatable fact that if this mere woman could locate him out in the middle of nowhere, the posse would undoubtedly be close behind. Before he could respond, her eyes fluttered shut again and her hand fell to her side. Wolfe shook her shoulders in an attempt to rouse her, and failed.

"Hell." Frustrated, he stood up, his hands braced on his hips and stared down at her. Nearby, his mare whinnied, as if reminding him that they didn't have all day.

The woman was a pitiful sight. Her long yellow hair was wet and matted, bruises marred her face and her bottom lip was rapidly swelling from a cut she'd received in the accident.

She was also too thin for his personal taste. Her breasts, barely covered by that immodest scrap of lace and silk were too small to make a decent handful, and her complexion, even for an Anglo, was too pale. Yet, even as he assured himself that he felt no attraction for this unconscious female, something about her inexplicably moved something deep inside him.

Sympathy? Perhaps.

Responsibility? Absolutely.

He glanced up at the sky, at the drenching rain that showed no sign of stopping. He looked back toward town, half expecting to see the armed posse riding toward him. But there was only the towering red rocks, the green trees and, of course, the rain.

Finally, he returned his gaze to the woman. To leave her here, at the mercy of the inclement weather, not to mention the wild animals that roamed the range, along with whatever else fate might have in store for her, would be unconscionable.

On the other hand, to take her back to Whiskey River, where she could obtain the medical attention she needed and deserved would ensure his recapture. And his execution.

His vexatious conscience warring with a deep-seated instinct for survival, Wolfe swore viciously. First in his native Navajo. Then in the language of the Anglos he'd learned to use to his own advantage in his writing.

Finally, knowing he had no other choice, damning whatever gods—or, more likely, devils—had dropped her into his life, he scooped up the troublesome female and flung her across the back of his patiently waiting mare. Viewing the leather satchel lying near where she'd landed, he picked it up, as well, glanced inside it and saw that it seemed to contain books, which made him wonder if she could be a schoolteacher.

He thought about the thin-lipped missionary teachers he'd suffered during his years away in boarding school. Then he thought of this woman's enticing undergarments. If she was a teacher, things had definitely changed since his school days.

Cursing himself for a fool, he swung up behind her and began riding in the direction of the Road to Ruin.

He'd hand off the woman, whoever she was, to Belle O'Roarke.

And then, his duty done, he'd get back to the business of saving his own life.

4

HAD THE ROAD TO RUIN been situated in the red-light
district known as Whiskey Row, Wolfe wouldn't have
risked returning. But Belle O'Roarke, to escape city
council regulations, had opened for business several
miles outside Whiskey River.

Her whores—often "fallen girls" from respectable
households back East—were famous for being the
prettiest, the most well-mannered, the best-dressed—
or underdressed—and most important, the cleanest
girls in Arizona Territory.

Breaking with tradition that tended to separate the
establishments catering to various sins, the Road to
Ruin had a saloon, a gambling hall and a bordello all
operating under the same roof.

The piano player was pounding out Scott Joplin's
ragtime when Wolfe carried his still-unconscious charge
up to Belle's kitchen door at the back of the two-story
frame building.

The madam herself opened the door at his first
knock.

"What the hell are you doin' here?" she asked, her
eyes wide in her rosy face. "I figured that if you did
manage to escape, you'd hightail it for the border."

"I was on my way out of town when I got sidetracked."

"So I see." Belle 'folded her arms across her abundant bosom, draped in emerald satin, and eyed the

woman flung over his shoulder. "I don't suppose she's meant for me?"

"I don't care what you do with her," Wolfe growled as he entered the steamy warmth of the kitchen that smelled of fresh-brewed coffee, wood burning, bacon frying and wet dog. "Just take her off my hands so I can get the hell out of here."

"Who is she?"

"I don't know."

Belle grabbed hold of a handful of wet hair and jerked Noel's head up. "That's a helluva knot on her head. What happened?"

"The fool ran her buggy into the path of my horse."

"She was by herself?"

"If she'd had a man to take care of her, I wouldn't be here," Wolfe said grumpily.

"You didn't have to stop in the first place," Belle reminded him.

"Yes." Wolfe sighed. "I did."

Despite the seriousness of the situation, Belle threw back her head and laughed. A ribald laugh that started way down in the gut and bubbled out as rich and warm as the hearty beef stew bubbling away on the back burner of the cast-iron stove.

"You always have had a tendency to play Sir Galahad."

Wolfe hated being flattered for something he considered a deep and vastly embarrassing personal flaw. "Why don't you just tell me where to put her?"

"Mary's off visiting her cavalry officer in Prescott. You know, I think there may just be a marriage brewing there." Belle grinned. She was not one to begrudge her girls happiness whenever and wherever they could find it. "We can use her room. We'd better go up the back stairs, though," she decided. "No point risking anyone seein' you."

He followed her up the narrow wooden servants' stairs and was making his way down the hall, when a door opened and a man came out of one of the bedrooms. Wolfe quickly turned toward the wall so as not to be recognized, but such evasive movement didn't prove necessary since Oliver Platt, president of the Whiskey River First National Bank and Trust, and founder of the Citizens for Decency League, scurried past in a dense cloud of bay rum, eyes directed to the carpet. Obviously, he was no more eager to be recognized than Wolfe.

The woman the banker had been with leaned against the doorframe and eyed Wolfe with amusement. "I don't remember you ever carrying me up those stairs, Wolfe." Beneath a peroxide fringe of yellow curls, the woman's brown eyes danced with amusement.

"I don't recall your ever needing carrying, Lucy," Wolfe answered. "Seems to me, you're usually dragging me upstairs."

"Only because a good man is hard to find," Lucy responded saucily. She put a red-tipped fingernail into her mouth, tilted her head and gave him a lusty look. "Or is that a hard man is good to find?" she mused aloud. "I always get those mixed up."

"You? Mixed-up?" Despite his dire circumstances, Wolfe laughed. "You've got a mind like a steel trap, Lucy, my love." He had, after all, seen her ledger book, where she kept diligent track of her earnings—deposited in an interest earning account in Oliver Platt's bank—earmarked to open a boardinghouse for miners in Jerome.

Feeling momentarily lighthearted, he bent his head and kissed her pouting rouged lips.

"I'd better get her into bed," Wolfe said when Noel moaned softly, garnering his attention.

"Doesn't look like she's going to be much good there," Lucy observed. "You get tired of playing nurse-maid, Wolfe, sweetie, you know where to find me." She ran her bloodred fingertips seductively down the side of his cheek. Then, with a rich laugh, she sauntered down the hallway toward the stairs, obviously intending to join the festivities in the saloon.

Hefting the unconscious woman a bit higher on his shoulder, Wolfe continued down the hall in the opposite direction.

NOEL'S HEAD was pounding and every bone and muscle in her body ached. Seeking relief from the pain, she shifted, feeling the cool rustle of satin sheets beneath her. A soft moan escaped her lips.

"She's coming to," she heard a woman say through the mist draping her mind. The sweet scent of lilacs and roses drifted closer, mingling with the pleasant aroma of juniper wood emanating from a nearby fireplace. Along with the unmistakable scent of wet dog.

"It's about time." Wolfe stroked a cool damp cloth across Noel's throbbing forehead. As she breathed in the soothing scent of lavender water, he continued to bathe her face, her neck, her shoulder blades. When he hit a tender spot, she flinched and moaned again.

"Shh." He pressed a fingertip against her lip, then brushed her hair back from her forehead with an infinitely tender touch that belied the rough calluses on his fingertips. "It will be all right." The cloth continued its soothing journey down her right arm, and then her left. "You will be all right."

Although it took an effort, she opened her eyes and looked directly into his. He was as dark, as handsome, as mesmerizing as he'd appeared in his photographs. He also looked too real to be a dream.

But what else could he be? The last thing she remembered was driving her car through the rain. Perhaps she'd crashed and suffered a head injury, and he was merely a hallucination.

"I realize this is a cliché," she managed to say through lips that were impossibly dry. "But could you please tell me where I am?"

His eyes narrowed. "You're outside Whiskey River. In Arizona Territory."

Territory. Not state. Noel noticed. "What year?"

He exchanged a quick look with the older red-headed woman standing beside him. "It's 1896."

This was impossible. He *had* to be a hallucination. She may have inherited Katia's gift of second sight, but Noel had never heard stories of her grandmother possessing the power to zap back and forth between centuries. Time travel? That was something for Jules Verne. For the crew of "Star Trek." Not for a serious, level-headed woman who'd always kept both feet firmly planted on the ground.

"It's 1896," she repeated, wanting to cling to the notion that somehow this was some hallucination born of a cracked skull. But she had the strangest feeling that it was all too true. "You must really be Wolfe Long-walker."

His indigo eyes revealed not a scintilla of emotion. No kindness. No concern. "I told you before. You have the wrong man."

"No." She shook her head on the satin pillow, wishing she hadn't when the gesture caused boulders to start tumbling around inside again. Her eyes drifted closed once more as she concentrated on overcoming the pain. "I don't." Although barely whispered, the words possessed an iron-clad certainty.

"You poor little thing," Belle said with obvious sympathy. "You must be hurtin' something awful."

"I've felt better," Noel allowed.

"Don't worry, we'll fix what ails you with a little laudanum."

The familiar word, which told her yet again that somehow she'd managed to land herself in the nineteenth century, infiltrated into Noel's consciousness. Although she felt as if she'd been run over by Burke's racing car, she had no intention of spending her honeymoon in some Swiss drug rehabilitation hospital. That being the case, the one thing she did know right now was that she certainly didn't want a dose of opium.

"No." Her lips formed the words, but she wasn't certain she'd said them out loud. "Please. I'll be fine."

Her faint protest proved unnecessary. About this, apparently, Noel and Wolfe were in agreement.

"There's another way." He reached into the suede pouch tied around his waist and took out a piece of white willow bark which he handed to the buxom madam. "Boil this into a tea. It will soothe her pain."

Belle shrugged. "If you say so. Though it seems like a lot of work to go to, when laudanum works just dandy." She left the room in a rustle of satin skirts.

This time, when she opened her eyes, Noel's gaze was filled with gratitude. "Thank you. You're very kind."

He shrugged. "I did not act out of kindness. There are already enough white women addicted to laudanum in

Arizona Territory. I see no point in adding to the population."

"Nevertheless, I appreciate it." Her formality matched his. She'd experienced more warmth suffering through boring royal dinners with visiting dignitaries.

Her lips felt dry and cracked. When she licked them, he looped a strong arm around her shoulder and lifted her to a sitting position, allowing her to drink from the glass he held up to her mouth.

The sheet slid away, revealing that someone had undressed her while she'd been unconscious. Embarrassed to have her bare breasts exposed to this man's heavily hooded dark eyes, Noel tried to remind herself that she'd grown up sunbathing on topless European beaches surrounded by strangers. When that didn't work, she tugged the sheet up to her chin and hoped it would stay there as she sipped the water he was offering.

The finest champagne from the Montacroix vineyards could not have tasted so exquisite, or have been so appreciated. The water slid coolly down her throat like a soothing waterfall.

"Thank you," she said again on a contented sigh as he lowered her to the pillow.

She'd felt soft and warm in his arms, reminding Wolfe, more than that shared kiss with Lucy, exactly how long he'd been without a woman. Furious at the way his mutinous body had betrayed him, aching from the blood that had flooded into his groin at the sight of those pale, perfect breasts, Wolfe set his jaw and frowned down at her. "I told you—"

"I know." Her refreshed lips curled into a soft smile. "Gratitude is unnecessary." Swallowing, this time to rid her throat of the strange lump of emotion that seemed to have settled there, she said, "However, it seems to me that when one person saves another's life, gratitude is in order."

"A cooling drink is hardly saving another's life."

"No. But we both know that I wouldn't have stood much of a chance if you'd left me out there in the mud and storm. With the wild animals. And heaven knows what the more unsavory members of that posse would have done if they'd come across me lying out there all alone. Without protection."

The thought, not a pleasant one, had already occurred to him. The idea of those ruffians from town—men more likely to be wanted for heinous crimes themselves—abusing her in ways no woman should ever have to suffer, was the reason he'd brought her to Belle's.

Hell, Wolfe figured grimly, if he didn't get out of here now, he may as well just ride back to town, stick his damn-fool head into the hangman's noose and be done with it.

Wolfe grunted. "What posse?"

"Don't do this." Ignoring the pain that jangled behind her eyes at the slightest movement, she sat up again and placed her hand on his arm. The muscle that tensed beneath her touch was as unyielding as a stone. It also matched the renewed hardness in his eyes. "I know that you're running from the law."

He plucked her slender white hand from his sleeve. "Probably half the territory knows that by now."

"I suppose they do. But I'm not from here."

Although he laughed at that, there was not a hint of humor in the rough sound. "I may just be an ignorant half-breed, sweetheart, but I figured that out for myself."

Noel had never possessed a temper. Chantal was the Giraudeau sister capable of fireworks. Yet the self-derision in his tone had her wanting to slap the sardonic smile off his lips.

"I've read one of your books." When he didn't answer, she said, *"Sand Paintings On A Hogan Floor.* The stories were incredible. They came alive for me."

"And now you've come to Whiskey River to meet the author."

"Yes. In a manner of speaking."

"In a manner of speaking," he repeated dryly.

Hell, this entire farce was only about sex, Wolfe thought disgustedly. He'd seen it before, too many times to count, women who got a sexual thrill from bedding a man they considered only a step above a wild animal—his namesake—then sharing exaggerated, scandalous tales over afternoon tea.

In the beginning, when he'd first begun traveling beyond Dinetah, the land of his people, he'd been flattered by the plethora of feminine attention. Stunningly beautiful, frighteningly aggressive women on two continents had shed their silks and satins, eager to sleep with a man so different from the ones in their privileged worlds. And Wolfe had enjoyed each and every one of them.

For a while. Then he realized that anything too easily attained became boring. The idea that he'd been used as some type of exotic savage had also stung his male ego, but he'd overcome it. As he'd overcome so much else in his past.

And on those rare occasions when the need for a woman built to an intolerably painful physical level, well, hell, that's what girls like Lucy were for. A quick roll between some hot sheets, then they both got on with their lives. No promises. No regrets.

"Since you've come all this way to meet me," he said in a low deep voice that rumbled in the stillness of the room like the threatening growl of a wolf, "I suppose it would be a shame to send you back to wherever you came from disappointed."

Before Noel could discern his intentions, his fingers tightened painfully on her chin and his unsmiling mouth swooped down like a hawk on a hapless, startled dove.

Noel instantly forgot her throbbing head as the fierce kiss drained her mind of all reason and stole the breath from her lungs. When she gasped at the impact, he took full advantage, thrusting his tongue deeply into her mouth. Fingers of flame curled through her, firing an instantaneous yearning that was as unexpected and unbelievable as this entire situation. His mouth was rough and hot and every bit as possessive as the dark hand that settled deliberately over her bare breast.

"Well," a rich contralto voice rang from the doorway, "looks as if you've found some other way to cure what ails the girl, Wolfe."

Belle's laughing voice had the effect of a bucket of icy water thrown onto a fire. Noel could practically hear the hiss and sizzle of steam rising from her heated flesh.

Wolfe had gone absolutely rigid. She suspected, rightly, that he was struggling to rein in his own out-of-control emotions. He cursed, an earthy curse Noel knew would survive another century.

He stood up, his back as rigid as his expression. The taste of desire had soured in his mouth. "Anyone ever tell you that you've got rotten timing, Belle?"

"Not as bad as you think," the older woman countered. "Lucy wanted to bring up this tea. Think what might've happened if she'd caught you swapping spit with some other female."

"Probably take a piece of hide off my ass. Then scalp me."

"At the very least." Belle cast a glance down at Noel. "I suppose we ought to introduce ourselves. I'm Belle."

Still in a bit of a daze from that devastating kiss, Noel managed a faint, polite smile. "My name is Noel."

"Now, ain't that a pretty name. For a pretty girl. And nothing personal, honey, but if you want to give it away, I'd prefer you do it somewhere else. This here's a working house and I've got too much dough invested in that bed not to get my share. So to speak."

"I didn't mean for that to happen," Noel insisted on a shaky voice far removed from her usual calm tone. She unconsciously lifted her fingers to her still-tingling lips. "I'm usually much more circumspect."

Now *that* was definitely the understatement of the century. Make that both their centuries, Noel thought miserably. What on earth had gotten into her? She'd never been so shaken by a mere kiss in her life. Not even when kissing Bertran.

Especially when kissing Bertran.

"Don't worry that pretty head about it," Belle said easily. "From the look of it, you and Wolfe here had yourselves quite an adventure. A little danger always tends to get the juices flowing."

"I believe I've heard the same theory," Noel agreed. As she dragged her hands through her hair, the sheet slipped down to her waist again. She pulled it back up to her chin, ignoring Wolfe's arched, mocking eyebrow. "It's the adrenaline rush, I believe."

"Wouldn't know about that." Belle shrugged. "But I do know that things always pick up around here after a gunfight in town. Why, just last month, Doc Holliday came through Whiskey River, and—"

"You going to give her that tea while it's still hot, Belle?" Wolfe suggested dryly. "Or keep cooling it with your tongue."

"This tea isn't the only thing that needs cooling off," the madam retorted. "Ain't like you not to watch your back, Wolfe. If I'd been one of those black-hearted bounty hunters, you'd be picking buckshot out of your ass right about now."

"I appreciate your efforts to keep me alive. And speaking of which, I'd better get going."

"Seems to me I said something about that earlier," Belle agreed.

He turned toward the door, ignoring Noel as if she no longer existed. As if that hot kiss had never happened.

"Wait!" Noel's heart lurched in her chest as she realized he was about to leave the brothel. "You can't. Not yet."

He folded his arms across his chest and flicked a remote, assessing look over her. "Look, sweetheart, you're an attractive woman. And hotter than a firecracker on the Fourth of July. But you see, I've got myself in a little fix right now and I can't risk hanging around here to scratch that itch you've come so far to ease."

"Is that what you think?" Once again, a temper Noel had not known she possessed flared. "You think this is all about sex?"

"We weren't exactly discussing the state of the Union a few minutes ago."

His dry tone and mocking eyes only caused her irritation to rise higher. "My reasons for coming to Whiskey River have nothing to do with making love to you, Mr. Longwalker."

"The name's Wolfe."

"So at least you're admitting who you are."

"Not much point in denying it. Since everyone around here seems to feel free to fling it around so easily. Yeah, I'm Wolfe Longwalker. And I'm also wanted for murder.

"So, if you don't mind, lady, I'm just going to be on my way. Maybe we'll meet up again one of these days, when I've got a bit more time, and finish this. In the meantime—"

He bent his head again and gave her a rough deep kiss that sent a renewed flare of heat shimmering through her like sparklers, all the way to her toes.

With that, he was gone. Noel sat there, her fingers pressed against her lips, where she could still feel the heat of his mouth, stunned that she'd come so far, only to fail now.

"You can't let him go!"

When she tried to jump out of the rumpled bed, Belle pushed her back against the pillows with a fleshy palm against the shoulders.

"No one tells that man what he can or cannot do. If he wants to head out to Mexico or Timbuktu, the entire U.S. Cavalry ain't gonna stop him."

"I have to save his life."

Even as she heard herself saying the words, Noel knew they were true. It was why, as impossible as it seemed, she'd somehow managed to slip through an invisible curtain of time, ending up here, in Whiskey River a hundred years in the past.

Belle stood beside the bed, still holding the cup of willow bark tea, looking down at Noel.

"No offense meant, honey, but if that was your way of trying to keep the man safe, I'd say your methods leave a bit to be desired." Belle shook her head. "It's not even a little bit safe for Wolfe to be hanging around the Road to Ruin. Not now. Not with every lawman and bounty hunter in the territory looking for him."

"You don't understand. It's not safe for him to leave here without me!"

Noel was appalled when she felt the hot sting of tears burning her eyes. She couldn't remember the last time she'd come close to crying. It was not her nature to allow her emotions the upper hand.

Belle's expression softened, giving Noel the impression that this was a woman accustomed to taking in strays. Girls, kittens and that mangy yellow dog that was standing beside the bed, looking up at Noel with what appeared to be canine adoration in its brown eyes.

"Why don't you just drink your tea," the older woman suggested. "You'll feel better."

What she needed was to get out of here. Now. So she could catch up with Wolfe. "So, he's left already?"

"He's gonna have himself a bite to eat first," Belle allowed. "But I don't think he wants company."

Your company. The madam left the words unsaid, but Noel would have had to have been deaf not to hear the qualification in the woman's tone.

She sipped the tea, considered her circumstances, and came to a conclusion. "If you don't mind," she said in a weak, fractured voice, "my head is really pounding. Do you think I might have just a touch of that laudanum, after all?"

"No problem." Belle nodded with robust satisfaction. "You'll see, honey, we'll get you feeling fit as a fiddle in no time." Her appraising gaze narrowed. "Nice ring."

Noel glanced down at the engagement ring she'd forgotten she was wearing. "Thank you."

"You got a fella to go with it?"

"I don't know," Noel answered honestly. "I'm supposed to get married, but . . . "

Her voice drifted off, but not before she was sure that Belle had caught the hesitation in her tone. The same hesitation she was certain Sabrina had detected. The same hesitation she'd been feeling ever since Bertran had slipped the diamond on her finger.

"I had myself a fiancé once," Belle revealed. "He was a traveling salesman. Sold notions. Needles, pins, playin' cards, tinware, everything from ladies' stockings to men's gaiters, calico to corn plasters, you got a use for it, my Fred would sell it to you."

"Bertran's a banker."

"A banker's bound to be a good provider," Belle responded with approval. "Dependable. And respectable. Bertran. Name sounds like a foreigner."

Dependable. Respectable. Both words described Bertran perfectly. "Yes, he is."

"Like you?"

"My mother's an American. But my father is European."

"I figured that, from your accent. Sounds French."

"You have a good ear," Noel murmured, not wanting to get into the particulars of her country.

"My piano player's a Frenchie. Used to play the music halls in Paris."

"I'm sure he's very good."

"Best in the territory," Belle agreed with a brisk nod of satisfaction. "This may seem like the back of beyond to a city girl," Belle said, "but a helluva lot of people make it out to the frontier. People lookin' for excitement. Adventure. People wanting to make a new life for themselves."

She gave Noel another of those long speculative looks. "I left poor old Fred standing at the altar in Philadelphia. Because I knew that I'd just dry up and blow away if I was forced to live the life other people had planned for me."

Although at first glance, this bawdy madam from a nineteenth-century whorehouse would seem to have little in common with a modern-day European princess, at that moment, Noel knew that beneath the skin, where it truly counted, she and Belle O'Roarke were more than a little alike.

"I've always done what was expected of me," she murmured.

"Until you up and came here to Whiskey River. Looking for Wolfe Longwalker," Belle guessed.

Despite the seriousness of the situation, Noel smiled. "Yes. Until I came here. For Wolfe."

A deep sigh caused the madam's bosom to rise and fall like a ship riding a swell at the pier. "He's a hard man to know. He'd be a harder man to love."

"Oh, I'm certainly not in love with him," Noel said quickly.

"Good. Because that would definitely be a road to ruin." Belle grinned at her intended pun as she patted Noel's arm. "I'll go get that laudanum. Then we'll decide what we're going to do with you."

She turned in the doorway. "By the way, I washed out your underwear in the basin after Wolfe and I cleaned you up. I've never seen the likes of it. You get those fancy drawers in France?"

The casually spoken statement about Wolfe assisting Belle in undressing her sent the color flooding into Noel's cheeks.

"Paris," she managed to say past the pulse that had begun jumping in her throat.

"I figured as much. Looks like I need to go on another shopping spree. Wouldn't want my girls not to have the latest fashions."

She winked broadly, then left the room.

The moment her emerald bustle sashayed across the threshold, Noel was out of bed like a shot, nearly tripping over the huge dog in her haste.

Ignoring the jagged pain behind her eyes, she began rummaging through the armoire in search of something to put on. Her slacks, denim jacket and blouse, still lying on the floor where they'd landed after Wolfe and Belle had undressed her, were still too wet to be wearable. Her bra and panties, freshly laundered, had been tossed over the back of a chair in front of the fire.

Unfortunately, the usual owner of this room did not share Noel's understated classical tastes. The armoire was filled with piles of frothy red-and-black lingerie and very little else. There was a maribou-trimmed robe, a royal-blue dress with a black lace petticoat with a scandalously—for the times—short skirt and a daring, beaded neckline that plunged nearly to the navel.

The only other dress in the armoire was definitely overkill— a scarlet-as-sin off-the-shoulder gown that while she feared would display a great deal of flesh would at least cover her legs. The dress was elaborately draped across the front of the skirt.

After putting on her underwear, she took the dress from its padded hanger and pulled it over her head. The material slid over her body like a silk waterfall, rustling like the wind in the trees. The deeply cut neckline displayed her pale breasts nearly to the nipples, revealing the lace at the top of her bra. Reminding herself that beggars couldn't exactly be choosers, Noel decided she had far more serious things to worry about at the moment.

Like figuring out how to save Wolfe Longwalker's neck.

She'd begun to pace, when she caught a glimpse of her reflection in a gilt-framed full-length mirror across the room. Coming to an abrupt halt, she was stunned by the transformation created by a few yards of material. She actually looked voluptuous. She looked, she thought with wonder, as sexy as Chantal. Although, Noel tacked on, her older sister's style sense had always leaned more toward elegant glamour, while this dress was admittedly, wonderfully, risqué.

"So," she said, turning toward the dog, who was sitting beside her, gazing up at her with a dopey look of admiration, "what do you think?"

When the huge tail began wagging like a metronome, Noel took it as a sign of canine approval.

Heavens, if her father could only see his younger daughter now, Noel considered, he'd undoubtedly think she'd lost her mind. Of course, he wouldn't be able to see her, she reminded herself. Since she'd left him and the rest of her family and friends, along with Bertran behind—or should she say "ahead" in the twentieth century.

Her head swam a little at the idea. As impossible as all this seemed, she sensed that she was not hallucinating. Nor was this another dream. She was here in frontier Arizona Territory, wearing a prostitute's dress designed to appeal to a man's most basic instincts.

And what about Wolfe's instincts? she wondered. Would he find her irresistible in this dress? And more to the point, why did she care?

DOWNSTAIRS, Wolfe dug into a bowl of beef stew. "Hanging around here is a damn mistake," he muttered darkly.

"Stopping to pick up that girl in the first place was the mistake," Belle said easily, refilling his coffee cup and placing a stack of fresh-baked bread in front of him. "You may as well stick around long enough to put some food in your belly."

"It's good stew," he grunted. Of course it was. Everything about the Road to Ruin was first-class. Which was what made the place the most popular sporting house in the territory. "Sticks to the ribs. You're a good cook, Belle. And a good woman. Generous. And warmhearted."

"What I am is a sucker for a good-lookin' man who ought to know better than to hook up with some foreign female while half the territory is on his tail."

"I told you—"

"I know. You didn't have any choice." She reached up to a shelf and took down a dark brown bottle of laudanum. "But we both know that's not the case." She looked across the room at him, then up at the ceiling, as if imagining the woman lying in Mary's bed. "I do have one question."

"What's that?" Wolfe began wiping up the dark gravy with hunks of bread.

"What am *I* supposed to do with her?"

He stopped for a moment, surprised by the question. He'd never stopped to consider the matter past getting her to Belle's, then continuing. "I suppose you could always put her to work."

"A girl like that'd probably draw men all the way from Prescott," Belle said. Watching the madam consider the idea, Wolfe could practically see the silver dollars piling up in Belle's coffers. "She's got a lot of class."

"For a fancy woman," Wolfe said grudgingly, irritated by the way the woman had, with a single kiss, expertly tied him up in sexual knots.

"She looks kinda like a princess from one of those fairy-tale picture books." Belle pointed out what Wolfe had already noticed on his own. She rubbed her three chins. "Maybe we can have an auction. For her first night."

He laughed at that. "If you were a man, Belle, you'd probably be running the Union Pacific."

"If I were a man, sweetie," she retorted, "I'd be running this whole damn country."

"I'd go for that." He stood up, tossing the napkin beside the empty bowl. A ten-dollar note joined it. "President Belle O'Roarke. It's got a nice ring."

"Speaking of rings, the girl's engaged to a banker."

Shutters came down over his eyes, effectively hiding his thoughts. "You were due to be hitched yourself when you came West," he reminded her. "A woman with marriage on her mind doesn't go running around the country all by herself, without the man in question. Especially not wearing those flimsy, see-through drawers." Drawers that were designed for a male to appreciate, Wolfe tacked on silently.

"That's kinda what I figured." Belle folded her arms across her chest. "So, if she decides to stay on, how much do you think I could get away with charging?"

For some reason, the question irritated him. "Why the hell ask me what some man would pay to bed her?"

"Because you've gotten a sample of what she's offering. I thought you might want to offer an opinion. Compare her to Lucy, maybe?"

"There's no comparison." The answer was quick and blunt and out of his mouth before he could call it back. Hell, just thinking back on that ill-timed kiss made him hard. And angry.

Belle dragged her hand over her mouth, but not before Wolfe caught sight of her knowing grin. She reminded him of a fat cat who'd just laid eyes on a freshly churned pitcher of cream.

Wolfe was about to assure her that if she was thinking about him actually bidding for the sexual attentions of that warm and willing blonde he'd left wrapped in those black satin sheets upstairs, she'd better think again. But before he could remind the madam that he wouldn't be around for any auction, the kitchen door suddenly burst open and Wolfe found himself facing the ugly business end of a pair of Colt .45 Equalizers.

"Aw, hell," he said through clenched teeth.

A day that had started out on a downhill slide had just gotten a whole lot worse.

5

UPSTAIRS, Noel examined her shoulder bag that Wolfe had fortuitously retrieved and was heartened to see that although her billfold had apparently either not made the journey across the century, or had spilled in the accident, Wolfe's reprinted stories, along with the *Rogues Across Time* had survived intact.

When she took the book out of the bag, she experienced that now-familiar tingling and realized that this oddly energized book was somehow responsible for her being here. In this time. She was relieved to find the gallery invitation stuck between the pages where she'd left it.

She was wondering how open-minded Wolfe Longwalker would be when she tried to explain her lifesaving mission, when there was a loud crashing sound from downstairs. The yellow dog immediately stopped trying to put its huge head beneath her hand, raised its head and began to bark.

"Shh."

She reached down and stroked the dog's fur. Whatever was happening, she doubted it would be good. Determined not to make Wolfe pay with his life for having saved her's, she scooped a pearl-handled derringer from the green marble dresser top and slipped it into a side pocket of the voluminous scarlet skirt.

"We have to be very, very quiet," she murmured to the dog, pressing a warning finger against her lips. "I'll go first and check things out."

When she realized she was discussing rescue plans in the bedroom of a whorehouse with a yellow mutt the size of a Mercedes, Noel couldn't help wondering if this was how Alice had felt when she'd fallen down that rabbit hole.

Unwilling to leave her bag behind, she grabbed it, put the strap over her shoulder and began creeping down the hall, vaguely aware of the intimate sounds coming from behind some of the doors. Her heart was pounding so hard and so fast in her ears, she couldn't believe that everyone in the Road to Ruin couldn't hear it. And although she was trying her best to move as silently as possible, the rustle of the silk dress seemed deafening.

Behind her, following instructions to the letter, the dog slunk stealthily along, his bushy tail extended straight out like a battle flag.

In the saloon, the French-born piano player was still pounding away on the ivory keyboard. A few of the whores were singing along merrily as they straddled the laps of miners and cowboys, coaxing money out of denim pockets with whiskey and wet kisses that promised nirvana to be but a gold piece away. The laughter was loud and boisterous over the sounds of cards shuffling and poker chips clicking.

When she reached the kitchen, Noel held up a warning hand to the dog and prepared herself to save Wolfe Longwalker's life.

WOLFE REMINDED HIMSELF that although he may be down, he wasn't out. At least not yet. He'd been in worse fixes. He figured if he lived through this, he'd be in more again. Life was like that sometimes, he thought fatalistically. Just one damn thing after another.

"Hello, Jack," he greeted the familiar swarthy face of the gunfighter, without revealing a hint of nerves. "If you're come for dinner, I can highly recommend the beef stew. Belle's outdone herself this time."

"You know damn well what I've come for, Wolfe," Black Jack Clayton growled.

Wolfe cast a surreptitious glance at the winchester carbine he'd foolishly left on Belle's breakfront. No doubt about it, he was obviously getting careless in his old age. Not that thirty-three was all that old, but he had managed to cram one helluva lot of living into those years, and if this old enemy had his way, he'd just reached the end of the line.

"I figure it probably has something to do with that price on my head." Appearing not to have a single care in the world, Wolfe leaned back in his chair as if settling back after a satisfying meal. "So how much is it?"

"Twenty-five thousand dollars. Dead or alive."

"Twenty-five thousand." Wolfe whistled softly. He slid a sideways glance toward Belle, who had not said a word. But who was, dammit, inching toward her heavy iron skillet. A frying pan against two revolvers. Obviously, she was thinking with her gilded heart instead of her head again.

"Belle, darlin'" he said quietly, "why don't you leave Jack and me alone. So we can get down to some serious negotiating."

"There's nothing to negotiate, Longwalker," the man growled. "You're goin' to glory today. Or more likely, given that you're a savage, hellfire."

Wolfe felt the familiar flare of temper at the aspersion cast on his mother's people, but forced it down. If there was ever a time for a cool head, this was definitely it.

"Always nice to be among friends," he drawled. "Never thought gilded wings were much my style, anyway." He shot another stronger look at Belle. "Go on, sweetheart. It'll be all right."

"I'm not gonna have you dyin' here in my kitchen, Wolfe Longwalker," she retorted with a furious toss of her henna-red head. "It's bad luck."

"They'll be no dying here today, Belle," Wolfe assured her. "The bounty's for dead or alive. I'm willing to settle for alive."

"What makes you think I am?" the other man asked. "You're not calling the shots here, Longwalker. I am."

Jack Clayton had gotten his start as an army scout before he turned to selling firewater to the Indians, rustling cattle and robbing trains. The last few years, he'd worked as a hired gun for those ranchers who'd begun to feel more and more under siege by sodbusters streaming west in their prairie schooners.

Wolfe knew Jack's heart to be as black as his nickname. And the gunslinger's aim was, unfortunately, a lot truer than his character.

"Seems you've got the drop on me," Wolfe said. "But I'm offering you a choice, Jack. You can try to make it into one of those lousy Beadle dime novels by shooting an unarmed man. Or you can retire to California with fifty thousand United States dollars in your pocket. It's your call."

Wolfe's firm lips slashed a white, wicked smile. "Think how many sweet-smellin' fancy women and how much whiskey a man could buy with all that money, Jack. Think of the pleasures."

As he watched those deadly eyes momentarily glaze over, Wolfe judged the distance to the winchester and decided that with just a bit more luck, he could make it.

He mentally ran through the motions, then, just as he poised like a diamondback prepared to strike a fatal blow, the entire plan fell apart.

An explosion burst into the kitchen—a wild, colorful whirl of red satin and yellow fur. While the dog leaped for Black Jack's throat, Noel pulled the derringer from her pocket and before she could consider whether or not her behavior was wise or even necessary, she squeezed the trigger.

Black Jack cursed. Loudly. Viciously. He stared at Noel in absolute disbelief, then crashed to the floor with a force that made the dishes on the pine table rattle.

The sharp sound still reverberating in her head, Noel stared in horror at the dark stain spreading across the man's shirt. She'd been aiming for his arm! But when he'd tried to knock away the dog, the bullet had entered his chest instead, apparently striking him in the heart, if all that blood was any indication.

"Good shooting, girl," Belle said approvingly as she tossed Wolfe the winchester. "Now, you two better hightail it out of here."

Wolfe looked down at the man sprawled on the kitchen floor. Then he glared at Noel, who'd begun to tremble. "What the hell did you think you were doing?"

The harsh tone, slicing at her like a steel-tipped whip, cut through her icy shock. "Saving your life."

"I was more than capable of handling that on my own." The mutt, excited by all the activity, was now prancing around, his hind legs like one of those damn dancing circus dogs Wolfe had seen in Russia during a book tour his publishers had sent him on.

"He was going to kill you. I was sent here to stop him!" Anger sizzled like water on a hot skillet. Forgetting about the body lying at her feet, Noel tossed her head and met his furious glower with a lethal glare of her own. "So the least you can do is not yell at me!"

"I'm not yelling, dammit!"

"You're both yelling," Belle had to raise her own voice to be heard over their's. "Which is a damn-fool thing to do considering how many of those cowboys out there would be willing to take you on for half that reward, Wolfe. Now, get out of my house. Both of you. I'll try to clean up the mess you've made."

Wolfe cursed ripely. He knew Belle was right about his need to get as far away from the Road to Ruin as fast as possible. But dammit, although she'd messed things up royally, he couldn't leave his well meaning but addle-headed savior behind.

It didn't matter that Black Jack had drawn first. Neither did it matter that the man was lower than a rattlesnake in a rut. The gunfighter had been hired by the ranchers. He had their protection. And around these parts, that meant the law was on Jack's side.

Knowing he'd never forgive himself if he allowed a noose to be put around that slender white neck, Wolfe grasped Noel's arm and dragged her out the kitchen door.

"I suppose it would be too much to hope for that you can ride a horse," he said tightly as he untethered his mare from the rail behind the house.

Whore or not, he'd never met a female who seemed more out of place in this rustic setting. Even in that outrageous red dress, she brought to mind gleaming electric chandeliers, heavily gilded mirrors and hushed, richly appointed sitting rooms furnished with ornately carved velvet-covered furniture.

"Actually, I'm an excellent rider."

"You damn well better be. Because you're about to add horse stealing to your crimes."

Without waiting for her permission, he grabbed hold of her hips and practically threw her into the Western-style saddle of Black Jack's horse hitched to the rail. She instinctively leaned forward to gather up the reins as he swung onto the back of the mare.

"And since that horse stealing just happens to be a hanging offense around here, let's try to get away without you messing things up again."

Her response was cut off by a loud shout coming from behind her. Looking back over her shoulder, Noel saw a man standing in the doorway.

At the same time that the first rifle shot cracked high above them, Wolfe wheeled his mount.

"Ride!" he shouted.

When a second shot splintered the wood of a nearby tree, Noel ducked her head and took off like the wind.

To cover her, Wolfe kept his mare behind Noel. Winchester in hand, he rode a zigzag path as bullets kicked up puffs of red earth all around them. When he felt the burn as one of those rapidly fired bullets grazed his arm, he urged the mare to run faster.

The horse's hooves pounded on the dry earth, thin trails of dust roiled just above the ground behind them as they galloped away from the Road to Ruin. Behind them, the clouds of gun smoke drifted away as Wolfe took the lead. With her heart pounding in her throat, Noel followed him into the woods.

The rain had stopped, a brisk breeze from the west had blown away the clouds, allowing sunlight to stream through the tops of the towering Ponderosa pine trees.

Wolfe cast a glance up at the sun and determined that it was not yet noon. And he'd already packed one helluva lot into a single morning.

When thirteen-year-old Brady Loftin had shown up at the jailhouse window, bringing word from Fat Nell down at the Branding Iron Saloon that a bunch of cowboys were getting liquored up and planning a little necktie party to lynch the "Injun" who'd cold-bloodedly murdered innocent settlers in their soft feather-beds, Wolfe had come to the conclusion that he'd overstayed his welcome in the territorial jail.

Breaking out had been a cinch.

Staying out hadn't seemed all that tough a problem. Until a lissome female had been dumped in his lap.

As they made their way through the woods, headed toward the relative safety of the reservation, Wolfe's mood, already blacker than coal dust, got even filthier. Thanks to this woman who'd literally fallen into his life, his situation had taken yet another deadly twist.

It was not easy sitting a horse with yards of scarlet silk piled up almost to her chin. It wasn't fun riding hell-bent for leather up the side of a steep cliff nearly as vertical as a stone castle wall back home. Fortunately, Black Jack's pinto proved both fast and surefooted, keeping up with Wolfe's mare as he took them both higher and higher up the Mogollon Rim, deeper and deeper into the forest.

It didn't take long for the adrenaline rush to fade. And when it did, the image of Black Jack began dancing in front of her eyes. Noel imagined she could still see the shock in those cruel dark eyes when he realized he'd been shot. Along with that bright red stain on the front of his grimy shirt. If that wasn't bad enough, she imagined she could smell the dark, dank scent of the gunfighter's blood.

Her stomach churned. She tried to ignore it, but the images grew more vivid, the gagging worse. Finally, unable to hold back another minute, she slid off her horse and dropped to her knees on the floor of pine needles. And threw up.

At the sound of her coughing and sputtering, Wolfe reined in and turned the mare and observed her, on her knees, bent over, as ill as a camp dog. Something moved inside him. Something he steadfastly ignored as he reached down and silently handed her a canteen.

If she'd been hoping for sympathy—which, Noel assured herself, she most definitely wasn't—she would have been disappointed. As she sipped the water, willing it to calm her rebellious stomach, she risked a glance upward. His eyes were every bit as expressionless as his lean sculpted face.

"Thank you," she murmured, handing the canteen back to him.

"Save your thanks for when we get away from here without getting killed." His tone was as hard as his flinty eyes. His dark glance swept over her dismissively. Then he clucked at the mare and turned away, leaving her to follow.

As the hours dragged on and the miles passed by, Noel became exhausted and sore and thirsty. Depression battled with pain and fatigue. Despite the fact that her behavior had been justified, never mind the fact that she would do it again in a heartbeat, the idea of having shot another human being hung heavily on her heart.

Hot tears stung at the back of her eyelids. She blinked them away. The always serene Princess Noel never cried. Ask anyone in Montacroix. Not that anyone currently living in her country would even know of her, she thought wretchedly.

Only days ago, she'd been comfortably living in her family's palace, preparing for her wedding. She'd been happy. Contented, which for her, had always been pretty much the same thing.

Since stepping into whatever time warp she'd somehow entered, she'd been thrown from a carriage, had suffered what well could be a concussion, had been mistaken for a whore, had shared a distressingly hot kiss with an escaped outlaw she'd just met, had shot a bounty hunter, then had stolen his horse.

Her family would never believe it.

She hardly believed it.

Which meant that if Wolfe Longwalker ever did stop riding long enough for her to try to explain her situation, he'd undoubtedly find the scenario preposterous.

"I'm beginning to have my doubts about this being a very good idea," she murmured to the horse, stroking the silky black mane as they settled down for a walk. Since that initial burst of speed when they left the Road to Ruin, they'd been maintaining a pace of walk, trot, canter, then walk again "But there's not much I can do about it now."

Which, of course, brought to mind another question. Having landed here in the first place, would she ever be able to return home? To her own country? And her own time?

The fancy lady had guts, Wolfe determined grimly as he guided the mare across ground that was as familiar to him as his own face. Except for that brief hot argument in Belle's kitchen, the woman hadn't opened her mouth once. And for a woman who, if that diamond ring and those pearl earrings were any indication, appeared to earn a very good living on her back, he had to admit that she sat tall in the saddle.

That she'd proven unafraid of confrontation did not surprise him. A lot of whores he'd met over the years tended to have violent natures. Fighting seemed to be as much their specialty as loving. He'd certainly seen more than one pair of bawdy-house belles come to blows over the favors of a man. He'd also witnessed a drunken bully ending up on the wrong side of a female's dagger for cheating her out of her rightly earned pay.

On the other hand, the violence didn't even out. Since the women were invariably smaller and weaker, they tended to end up on the losing end of most physical battles between the sexes.

Unless, of course, Wolfe amended, they were armed with a derringer, as this one had been. Thinking back to that expression of utter shock and disbelief on Black Jack's face when he realized he'd been shot, almost made Wolfe smile.

Almost but not quite. Not yet.

He cast a glance upward at the sun, gauging time and distance. And continued.

Noel desperately longed to stop. But Wolfe continued to set a grueling pace, backtracking, riding the horses in the shallow waters along the banks of Whiskey River to throw their pursuers off the track. And since she had the feeling that there was absolutely nothing she could say to make him take a break, she had no choice but to follow his lead. Although he seemed to know exactly where he was going, she could not pick out any discernible trail.

Keeping single file, they threaded through a series of narrow canyons, headed toward the top of the mesa. Every so often, a loose stone skipped away from beneath a hoof and scattered downward, landing with a clatter on the rocks below.

Only sheer determination kept her in the heavy, unfamiliar, high-backed saddle. Her bottom ached, and her thighs, bare beneath the silk skirts, felt as if they'd been rubbed raw.

Finally, she had to ask. "Can't we stop?" she called out, ducking to avoid a tree branch that threatened to take off the top of her head. Her tongue was literally sticking to the roof of her mouth. "Just for a little while?"

"No."

The single word was flat and final. He didn't even bother to glance back at her. Indeed, if anything, he picked up the pace, urging his horse to a canter. Cursing in a very unprincess-like way, Noel picked up the pace and rode after him.

She didn't believe he'd leave her out here in the wilderness all alone, not after having already saved her life. And surely not after she'd saved his.

But she wasn't quite ready to put it to the test.

Wolfe glanced up at the sky again, almost unconsciously calculating the time until sundown. Although he'd spent much of his life among the whites, he'd been born with the iron stamina of the Dineh and could travel for days without sleep.

Before he'd been sent away to that hated white man's boarding school in the East, back when he'd still lived with his mother's sister's family, in the warm red heart of Dinetah, Wolfe had heard stories of how the elders had been capable of covering a hundred miles a day, and more.

His own mother's father had reminisced about the days when members of raiding parties would run their horses into the ground, then dismount and run.

During the *Naahondzond*—the Fearing Time—when the hated Kit Carson, known to The People as the Rope Thrower, had tried to kill off every Navajo in Arizona Territory, the outgunned Dineh had been forced to hide among the canyons. His grandfather had told of several instances of going seventy-two hours without sleep, much of it in the saddle.

But that had been desperation. This was reality.

He knew she had to be exhausted. Still, better to be exhausted, Wolfe reminded himself, than dead.

The sun was sinking below the jagged mountain peak to the west in a blazing display of crimson and gold. As dusk settled over the land, spreading deep purple shadows, Noel decided that things had gone on long enough.

She didn't care if the entire U.S. Cavalry caught up with her, not that she'd caught so much as a glimpse of any pursuers. She'd worry about being captured—and, heaven help her, hanged— when and if the occasion presented itself. Right now, she was getting down from the back of this horse while she could still move a muscle in her aching body.

Before she could insist that she could not ride another moment, Wolfe reined in his horse. "We'll stop now."

"So soon?" she asked with atypical sarcasm. Princess Noel Giraudeau de Montacroix was never sarcastic. Never!

Wolfe shrugged, vaguely irritated at the way he found himself enjoying her acid tone. The fancy lady's fragile blond looks might give the impression of sugar and spice, but down deep, where it counted, she had a steel core.

Just like him.

"You could have stayed back at Belle's. Upstairs, where you belonged," he said pointedly.

"I belong with you."

That earned a weary sigh as he dismounted and walked a few feet away, lay on top of a low rise and trained a pair of field glasses on the vast valley.

"Do you see anyone?" she asked.

"No." He took another quick perusal, then, not wanting to chance that a stray glint of polished lens would betray their presence, he stood up and returned the field glasses to his saddlebag.

When she began to dismount, afraid she'd become hopelessly tangled in the voluminous skirts, Wolf caught her around the waist and lifted her easily to the ground.

It was then that she discovered her legs had about as much consistency as water. "Thank you."

She continued to hold on to his upper arms, afraid she'd embarrass herself by crumbling into a pile of red silk if forced to stand on her own.

Beneath her fingertips, the muscles in his arms felt like boulders. She would not have guessed that a man who earned his living writing could have been so fit. So hard.

Wolfe didn't say anything. Instead, he was looking down into her face with those brooding dark eyes that had the power to stop her breath in her lungs.

They stood there for a long suspended moment, close together, his firm thighs crushing the front of her dress, his long dark fingers creating a scorching heat at her waist, him looking down at her, her looking up at him.

Unnerved, she managed to drag her gaze from his. It was then she saw it. A bright red stain on the shoulder of his shirt.

"You've been shot!"

He shrugged, feeling the tug of sensitive flesh as he did so. "It's nothing."

"Don't be so ridiculously macho." Always feeling more at ease when she was in charge of a situation, Noel placed her hands on her satin-clad hips. "Take off your shirt."

Wolfe smirked to keep her from seeing that the concern he sensed beneath her feminine determination made him uncomfortable. "I like a lady who takes the direct approach." He unbuttoned the shirt and tossed it onto a nearby stump. "Want me to get rid of the pants, too?"

If it weren't for that flinch of pain he'd tried so hard to conceal, Noel would have hated him for behaving so crudely. It also took all her concentration not to be distracted by the hard copper wall of his chest.

"That won't be necessary," she answered mildly. The blood had dried into a brown crust, making it impossible to see what she was dealing with. Taking the canteen, she began pouring water over the wound.

"You waste too much of that and you're going to get real thirsty, real soon," Wolfe said, thinking of the vast miles of high desert they'd cross before reaching sanctuary.

"Surely we can get more from the river," she said calmly. "Besides, I need to see what type of wound we're dealing with."

"Have a lot of experience with bullet wounds, do you?" Wolfe wouldn't have been surprised if there'd been a few shots exchanged by drunken cowhands on a Saturday night over such a woman.

"Not that much . . . All right," she admitted, intimidated by his unblinking, steady stare. "None at all. But I've taken Red Cross training."

When that only earned an arched, questioning eyebrow, she elaborated. "First aid. It's a basic level of healing."

She began breathing easier when she was able to see the wound more clearly. "The bullet seems to have only grazed the flesh."

He glanced uncaringly at the furrow that had been carved through his skin. He'd had worse. Much, much worse.

"I told you it was nothing."

"True. But if you'd been wrong, you would have missed the opportunity to say I told you so. Because you would have been dead."

"Everyone dies. Sooner or later."

"True. But personally, I'd prefer later." She was about to hand him back his shirt, when she gasped at the sight of the raised flesh running down the front of his forearm. "What's that?"

He glanced down at the thick bands of scar tissue he'd forgotten about. "A little souvenir from a youthful tussle with a bear."

"A bear?"

He saw the horror move in waves across her face and realized that she was seeing him not as the writer of all those popular western books, but as a primitive, violent savage.

"We had a dispute over territory."

"Who won?"

"If I'd lost, I wouldn't be standing here with you today." He'd killed the mean-tempered bear, but it had cost him months of recuperation. That he'd managed to do so with only a knife had gained him a measure of fame among the Dineh, but that meant little to him now. During his thirty-some winters on this earth, he had seen far worse things than a bear claw.

She glanced around, more concerned about the idea of wild animals than of the posse that was undoubtedly after them. "Do you think there might be bears around here?"

"Might well be." He shrugged. "Probably some wolves, too. But don't worry, sweetheart, I'll keep them from eating you up."

Her strange day had been an unsettling experience. Noel was exhausted. And sore. Not being in the best of moods, the careless endearment rankled. "My name is not sweetheart. It's Noel."

He shrugged. "Whatever you want."

It was his experience that fancy women tended to change names about as often as they changed towns. This time next month she'd probably be Sassy Sally. Or Diamond Doll.

Although, now that he thought about it, she'd chosen well. The name, bringing up thoughts of sleigh bells, crystal snowflakes and the rich mulled wine he'd been introduced to in London, definitely fit.

Her nerves stretched. Tangled. Twisted into painful knots.

That familiar look she'd seen in his eyes—upstairs in the Road to Ruin—returned. His harsh lips quirked in a faint, almost self-mocking smile as he caught her chin between his fingers.

Her body was vividly aware of his nearness, responding to it in instinctively feminine ways as old as time. Warming. Softening. Feeling as rooted to the spot as the towering cottonwood trees that lined the riverbank, Noel held her breath and waited.

His harshly cut mouth was within a whisper of hers. She could feel his breath, warm and enticing, on her lips. She drew in a ragged breath intended to calm. It didn't.

Suddenly, without any warning to either one of them, emotions she'd reined in for too long—wild, confusing, distressing feelings—broke free inside Noel. And she burst into tears.

6

"WHAT THE HELL?" Wolfe's head jerked back and he let go of her as if he'd been burned.

"It's nothing." She turned away and covered her face in her hands. "Really." Having always been the family conciliator, even now, after all she'd been through, as distraught as she was, Noel's instincts were to try to smooth over this latest disaster. "It's just that everything's so confusing," she said through her sob. "And you've been d-d-dragging me through these woods all day, and I'm hungry and tired and I d-d-don't know what I'm doing here, and—"

"The only reason you're here with me is because you went off half-cocked and shot Black Jack Clayton," Wolfe told her gruffly. Like most men, he was impatient with things he couldn't control. And a female's tears definitely fit that undesirable category. "It's not exactly like I was looking to be slowed down by some damn fancy woman! Hell, we'll be lucky if either one of us escapes the hangman now."

"I'm not a fancy woman! Or a whore, or a prostitute, or a soiled dove, or any other euphemism you may prefer to use!"

She whirled back, her hair swirling around her bare shoulders with the sudden movement. Her bottom lip trembling, a torrent of tears began streaming down her face.

How dare he be angry at her? It wasn't as if she'd asked to come to nineteenth-century Arizona Territory! And she certainty hadn't begged him to take her to the Road to Ruin. But it wouldn't have mattered, anyway, she suspected, because this entire sequence of events had been set in motion when she'd first opened her sister's invitation.

Possibly even before that. Something, after all, had made Chantal choose that particular woodcut for her invitation.

"And as for shooting that horrid Black Jack person, I was trying to save your miserable life, Wolfe Longwalker, though Lord knows why. I should have just let him murder you right there in Belle's kitchen."

She drew in a deep ragged breath as she wiped furiously at her tears with the back of her hands. "And, just for the record, I'll have you know, that gunfights and hangings might be part of your normal frontier life, but the only thing I've ever shot at in my life were clay pigeons with my brother, Burke, back home in Montacroix. And I've certainly never—ever—killed a man!"

Her voice went up on a ragged wail as a new flood of tears burst forth. She, Her Serene Highness, Princess Noel, a common, garden-variety murderer. It didn't matter that she was trying to save Wolfe. The ugly truth was, she'd willingly taken the life of another human being.

"I can understand how you may have found the experience unpleasant," he agreed with a calm that caused her own emotions to flare even higher. And hotter. "Although, believe me, sweetheart—"

"My name is Noel!" That she was shrieking at him was as unbelievable as everything else that had occurred.

His nod was curt. Brusque. Acknowledging her point without conceding an inch. "Believe me, *Noel*, there isn't a person alive, including Black Jack's mother, who'll miss him. He was a cold-blooded, low-life son of a bitch who'd just as soon shoot a man—or beat up a woman—as look at them."

"Still, he was a human being." She closed her eyes in an attempt to block out the memory of that fatal blood staining the front of the man's shirt. "Who's dead because of me."

"That's true enough, so far as it goes." Wolfe doubted anyone would show up at the graveyard to mourn the gunslinger. "But why blame me? I don't recall asking you to pull that trigger."

Noel wondered yet again how it was that he could remain so disgustingly calm when she was so horribly rattled. "I suppose I should have let you die?"

His eyes turned hard as stones. "You should have let me handle things. In my own way."

"Your way was about to get you a one-way ticket to boot hill."

Prepared for a scathing response, Noel was stunned when he suddenly threw back his head and laughed. A rich deep sound that warmed her unwilling heart and strummed innumerable chords deep inside her.

Embarrassed, needy, not to mention still terribly upset, she folded her arms across the crimson bodice of her dress and turned away again, looking out over the swiftly flowing waters of Whiskey River.

"Excuse me if I don't find dying very humorous," she said stiffly.

Wolfe cursed inwardly, wondering how on earth she had survived this long on her own in the rough-and-tumble world she'd chosen for herself, while seemingly remaining so damn sensitive. Once again, it crossed his mind that she wasn't like any whore he'd ever met.

"I didn't intend to insult you," he said. "It's just that part about boot hill sounded an awful lot like something out of a dime novel."

The suppressed laughter in his tone only irked her more. "We can't all be internationally famous writers."

"True." He found himself enjoying the bite of sarcasm edging her tone, preferring it to female tears any day.

He came up behind her and ran his palms across her bare shoulders. "Would it make you feel any better if I told you how much I appreciate your noble gesture?"

"Perhaps." She shook her head, trying to ignore the pleasure his massaging fingers were creating as they eased the knots out of her neck muscles. "It's just that it's all so difficult to take in. I keep trying to remind myself that only yesterday I was in Montacroix—"

"Impossible." He turned her around and looked down at her uplifted face, searching the depths of her eyes for some sign of a head injury. "That is a journey of several weeks."

"Not if you fly."

"Fly?" If she hadn't injured her brain in that accident, she was definitely addled, he decided. "Like that?" He pointed up at a red-tailed hawk that was flying wide lazy circles in the sky.

"Not exactly. I flew in a plane," she qualified.

"A plane." His tone was flat and absolutely disbelieving. She may as well have told him she'd donned a pair of gilt wings and gone soaring around the sun.

Noel sighed, deciding not to even mention the Wright brothers at this point in their conversation. "It's a bit like a train. With wings."

"Ah." He nodded. "Of course. A plane. So much more convenient than crossing the sea by ship," he said dryly. "I take it your home is in Montacroix?"

"Yes." Pleased that he'd recognized the name of her country, Noel allowed herself to believe that perhaps he would believe her outlandish story, after all. "My family rules Montacroix."

And had since a long-dead Giraudeau relative had purchased the Alpine principality from the French shortly after Napoleon's disastrous Russian campaign. With the treasury nearly depleted from having financed all those wars, the French government had sold off parcels of land to various noblemen.

She was as mad as a horse who'd gotten into a patch of locoweed, he thought. "I suppose that would make you a princess." Although his face remained expressionless, she could detect the sarcasm in his tone. A sarcasm, she decided, for now, to ignore.

"That's right. My sister Chantal, is also a princess. And my brother is regent."

"I met the regent of Montacroix last year," he informed her. "After a visit to Paris. And unless your parents spaced their children fifty years apart, there is no way that old man, Prince Leon, could be your brother."

"Well, of course he's not my brother," Noel agreed immediately. "My brother is Prince Burke. Well, actually, if you insist on getting technical, I suppose you'd have to say he's my half brother. You see, my father, Prince Eduard, had been married before, but his wife,

Princess Clea, went insane, and had to be institution-alized—"

"It appears insanity runs in the family."

Noel gave him a hurt, disapproving look, then continued, "Anyway, my papa met *maman*, who was an American movie star from California—"

"A star?" First, flying. Now, constellations. Wolfe wondered if the so-called princess had been spending a bit too much time in opium dens.

"A star is like an actress. Only bigger. More famous. My sister-in-law, Sabrina, is also an actress."

"And a princess, as well, I suppose?"

"Well, yes, but not by birth. She married my brother, which automatically makes her a princess, even if she is an American. From Tennessee."

"Sabrina the Confederate princess," he drawled. "This is becoming more and more fascinating."

This time, she would have had to be deaf to miss the blatant disbelief in his deep mocking voice. Noel sighed, realizing that she wasn't going about this at all the right way. Because every time she tried to explain how she'd come to be here, in this place, at this time, she'd get sidetracked and he'd never understand that she'd traveled a hundred years to save his life.

The thing to do, she decided, garnering as much of her characteristic practicality as possible under these outlandish circumstances, was to start at the beginning. With the invitation.

"I recently received an invitation," she said. "From my sister."

"The princess Chantal."

"Yes. She's an artist and the invitation was to a gallery showing in Washington, D.C."

"I thought your family was from Montacroix."

"We are." She exhaled a long frustrated sigh. "But Chantal lives with her husband in Washington. He used to guard the president," she said with a measure of family pride.

"Better and better." She had some imagination. He'd give her that. "So you received an invitation from your princess sister who lives in Washington where her husband guards presidents."

That wasn't exactly right, since Caine had resigned from the presidential security detail and had established a private security firm before proposing to Chantal, but determined to remain on track, Noel merely nodded.

Wolfe arched a dark eyebrow. "Was this before or after you flew here from Montacroix in the flying train?"

"Before. And it wasn't a train. I told you, it was an airplane. An Air France jet, actually, but that's not important right now, because if you don't let me tell this in my own way, we're going to be here a very long time."

"We're going to be here all night however you tell your story." Putting his hand against her back, he led her to a secluded spot beneath an outcrop.

Although it was spring, nights in the Arizona high country could be cold. Wolfe took the time to gather some wood and make a fire.

He also extracted some dried venison from his saddlebag. "Here. It is undoubtedly not what you are accustomed to dining on in your palace, but it is all I have."

"Thank you." The meat was tough. And basically tasteless. But it soothed the hunger pangs.

As she ate—quickly, as if she'd been starving—Wolfe pulled some tobacco from his suede pouch, poured it into a cigarette paper, rolled it up, struck a match with his thumbnail and lit it.

"Go ahead, Scheherazade," he invited, leaning back against the rocks. "I'm waiting with bated breath for the rest of this story."

Twenty minutes later, Wolfe was trying to convince himself that there was a logical explanation for the fact that this woman was in possession of books he'd written, all of which bore a reprint copyright date of 1996. Along with another book of biographies entitled *Rogues Across Time*, which stated he'd been hanged after a failed escape attempt in 1896.

Needless to say, Wolfe was not thrilled by that allegation.

He lit another cigarette, took a long puff of the smoke, held it in his lungs, then exhaled it on a series of white rings.

"I've seen a great many confidence schemes in my day, Princess. But I'll be damned if I can figure out what you're up to."

"It's not a scheme."

He frowned as he picked up the engraved invitation again, and studied the scene depicting Indians on horseback watching a log cabin go up in flames.

This was how it would have looked, he considered grimly. The day that unlucky settler family had been so cold-bloodedly killed. Anger stirred hotly in his gut. Anger at the murderers who appeared to have gotten away with their crime. Anger at the fact that people would be so willing to believe that he was a savage capable of committing such a heinous crime.

"You expect me to believe you have traveled from Montacroix, from a hundred years in the future, to save my life."

"And clear your name."

He shook his head. "The idea is impossible."

Noel had not expected this to be easy. His eyes were as black as the sky overhead. "That's what I thought, too," she admitted. "In the beginning. Because although I've grown accustomed to having inherited Katia's gift—"

"Katia's your Gypsy grandmother," he recalled, still trying to sort out all the family members she'd told him about. "Who your grandfather fell in love with during a holiday in Arles."

"After his graduation from Cambridge," Noel agreed. "Unfortunately, my great-grandfather Leon— the one you met—did not approve of the match. When he discovered that Grandfather Phillipe had married Katia, he threatened to disinherit him."

"Which he couldn't do. Because of the male line of ascendancy to the throne."

"Exactly. So you do know a bit about my home."

"I told you, I have visited Montacroix. It is a lovely country."

It also crossed his mind that her accent reminded him of the ones he'd heard while traveling in the small Alpine principality. Of course, Wolfe reminded himself, even if the woman was from Montacroix, that didn't necessarily mean that the rest of her outlandish tale was true.

"My country is the most beautiful in all Europe." Noel's pride in her homeland was more than a little evident. "Of course, it's not nearly as vast as America, and the people aren't nearly so diverse as they are here, but—"

"Let's get back to Grandfather Phillipe," Wolfe suggested.

"I'm sorry. I don't understand what's gotten into me. I'm usually much more to the point."

Wolfe decided that she was really quite endearing when she was trying to be earnest. He looked at the remains of the cigarette, its end but a cylinder of light gray ash. "I would imagine traveling across centuries might disrupt one's normal rhythms."

"Believe me, I've already discovered that for myself." Noel sighed. "Anyway, once my father, Eduard, was born, Great-Grandfather Leon immediately welcomed Katia and Phillipe back into the fold. With the birth of a male child, the country's future was assured, so Leon stepped down and allowed my grandfather to ascend the throne."

"And now your brother rules Montacroix," Wolfe recalled her saying. "His name is Burke?"

"Yes." Her smile was quick and bright. "When I left, he and Sabrina had just gotten word that they were to be parents."

She'd been awakened in the middle of the night by the sound of a newborn infant crying. A vision of the little boy was destined to become a Giraudeau.

"Phillipe's ascension to the throne was not without its detractors in the beginning," she revealed. "Since many people considered Katia to be a witch. Because of her clairvoyance."

"I can see how that might be the case." He ran his fingers around the gold-deckled edge of the invitation again and tried to remind himself that what she was suggesting was madness. "And you claim to have inherited this Gypsy gift of second sight."

"Yes." She lifted her chin, daring him to deny what was as much a part of her as her blue eyes or blond hair.

"Clairvoyance is one thing," he said, willing to forgo challenging her on that point. He'd heard stories of people from his own Bitter Water Clan who possessed the ability to foresee future events. Indeed, his mother's sister was one of the gifted people. "However, this tale of time travel is more difficult to swallow."

"It hasn't exactly been a cakewalk for me, either," she muttered.

Wolfe couldn't help chuckling at her dry tone.

"I'm so pleased you're finding all this amusing."

Her haughty tone contrasted intriguingly with her rich, throaty voice. "You know, Princess, whenever you pull out that empress-to-peasant tone, I almost believe you."

"I never lie."

The flash of temper in those lake-blue eyes and the aggressive thrust of her chin reminded Wolfe that this pretty blonde was no pushover. She may look about as soft as a feather bed, but the way she hadn't hesitated pulling the trigger on that derringer proved she was tougher than she looked.

She was also, he reminded himself firmly, a distraction he didn't need.

The grim amusement in his gaze faded to concentration as he returned to studying the invitation. "I recognize the artist," he said thoughtfully.

"Really?" This was even better than she'd hoped.

"His name is Bret Starr. Drinks too much and can't bluff worth a damn at poker, but he's got talent."

Excitement shimmied up her veins. Finally, evidence that her instincts were correct! That the invitation was the key.

"Do you think he actually witnessed the massacre?"

"I suppose that's possible." Wolfe rubbed his jaw and stared out over the rushing white water as he considered the possibility.

"If Bret Starr was there when the cabin was burned and that family killed, he could testify for you," Noel said excitedly. "He could clear your name!"

Her eyes were bright with hope and her cheeks were flushed again, but this time from sheer excitement rather than embarrassment. She was the loveliest woman he'd ever seen and if she wasn't really a princess, Wolfe decided she should be.

"What makes you think that I didn't massacre those people?"

"You didn't." Although admittedly, she may be confused about a great many things, on this all-important issue, Noel knew that she was standing on very firm ground.

"There are a great many people in the territory who would disagree with you."

"Then a great many people in the territory are idiots."

A ghost of a smile hovered at the corner of his lips. "Are you always this mule-headed?"

"Actually, Chantal has the reputation for tenacity. But since receiving that invitation, I've discovered that I possess a bit of that personality trait myself."

"I'd say *a bit* is putting it mildly." Especially if she'd come across time. Hell, Wolfe thought with a healthy burst of self-derision, now she had him considering the impossible.

"I have no intention of allowing you to be hanged." She leaned forward with a rustle of satin. "Don't you see? The invitation is the key."

"Don't go getting your hopes up."

He wondered who he was warning—her or himself. Saving his neck had been his first priority when he'd broken out of the Whiskey River jail. He hadn't allowed himself to even think about the possibility of clearing his name.

"Even if Starr was anywhere near Whiskey River at the time of the raid," he said, "it's more than likely that he was too drunk to make a credible witness."

"We won't know that for certain until we question him."

"We?" His voice was quiet. Deadly quiet and laced with a firm masculine warning.

A warning Noel chose to ignore. "We," she repeated firmly. She folded her arms beneath her breasts. "I understand from my reading about you that you are, by nature, a loner. However, now that I've killed that horrible Black Jack person, like it or not, Wolfe Longwalker, you're stuck with me."

He gave a snort that could have been a laugh. Or a curse.

"I can't figure out which of us is crazier," he muttered with a weary shake of his head. "You for thinking you're my guardian angel. Or me for starting to find the idea of being stuck with you rather appealing."

He said it quietly, his dark, dangerous eyes on hers. "I am, however, having no trouble understanding why your grandfather Phillipe risked a kingdom for his Gypsy, Katia."

As their eyes met across the dancing orange flames of the fire, Wolfe saw the rising desire in her gaze and realized that whichever she was—whore or princess—

a sexual involvement would complicate matters even more than they already were.

"You'd better get some rest," he said. "We have a long ride still ahead of us tomorrow."

He stood up, strode over to his horse and retrieved a bedroll.

"Are we going to Mexico?" She'd seen such an escape route often in the movies. "Or South America, like Butch Cassidy?"

"South America?" His expression revealed that he found this idea as outrageous as her claim of time travel. "Butch never went to South America."

"Not yet. But he will. With the Sundance Kid, and they'll be reported dead, but some people will believe that it was a ruse to throw the law off their trail so they could return to the United States and go straight."

He shook his head. "I'll say this for you, Princess. If you're *not* telling the truth, you have one hell of an imagination."

"I've done a great deal of reading about old-time outlaws," Noel explained. "Anyone who knows me could tell you that I've always been fascinated with the American West."

"Unfortunately, all those people who could collaborate your story happen to live a hundred years in the future," he said with lingering skepticism. "However, I think we'll skip South America. For now."

"So where are we going?"

He debated telling her. She seemed honest enough. But there were lots of outlaws who'd gone to the gallows after making the mistake of trusting a pretty face.

"How about I tell you when we get there?"

He didn't trust her. Noel's heart sank a little at the thought, but she had to admit that if she were in Wolfe's position, she might want to keep her getaway plans secret, too.

"Fine." The adrenaline rush was wearing off, leaving her both physically and mentally exhausted. "I think, perhaps, I'd like to rest my eyes. For a few minutes." She curled up on Wolfe's bedroll and instantly fell asleep.

Not willing to risk being captured while his guard was down, Wolfe remained awake, senses alert, as he watched her.

She was obviously wrung-out. And no wonder, considering what she'd been through. Even discounting that outrageous story about her having come from another time. Such things, he told himself, were impossible.

And yet . . .

Didn't the Navajo Story of Creation—told during the most sacred of ceremonials, the nine-day Blessing Way—trace his tribe through four distinct underworlds, until they emerged in this Fifth World, fully evolved with the assistance of the gods, into the people they were today. And didn't that same oral tradition teach that above this world was yet another, where all things blended with the cosmos?

Taking that into consideration, was it impossible to suggest that this woman's story, as outlandish as it might seem, could well be true?

He sat watching the fire. Flames danced restlessly, sparks would climb a few feet into the air, where they'd hang for a few moments, like stars, before winking out. Suddenly, Wolfe spotted a movement out of the corner of his eye, and leaped to his feet, revolver drawn.

"Aw, hell." He shook his head in disgust as the yellow dog from Belle's kitchen came out of the bushes, huge bushy tail wagging an enormous canine hello. The dog gave him a brief, dismissing glance, then, with a low, pleased moan, settled down next to the woman he'd obviously decided to adopt as mistress.

This was all he needed. For a man who'd always preferred to make his own way through the world, now he was suddenly stuck with two unwanted traveling companions—a woman and a butt-ugly yellow dog.

Deciding that he must have really angered ancient gods, Wolfe sat down again and reread his biography in the weathered *Rogues Across Time* by the flickering orange light, finding the story of his death no more palatable now than the first time he'd skimmed the pages.

His alleged hanging was what his princess was so anxious to change. Since so many other facts in the chapter were uncannily correct, Wolfe found himself idly hoping she could do it.

Which only proved, he supposed, that madness was contagious.

Cursing under his breath, he picked up the invitation once more. As ridiculous as he knew the idea to be, as he ran his fingers over the gilt-deckled edge again, Wolfe considered the very real fact that he might be holding his freedom in his hands.

Time passed. The night grew quiet. Not even a coyote broke the silence.

Determined to keep himself awake, Wolfe placed several sharp stones under his blanket so that the points dug into his back and shoulders, and the backs of his legs.

He stared up at the stars that glittered like so many hard, cold fires against the black sky, and listened to the rushing of water and the singing of crickets, punctuated now and then by the lonely hoot of an owl in a nearby tree.

"Who, indeed?" he murmured as he passed the night wondering about the woman who was sleeping just a few feet away.

When the sky turned a pale, predawn silvery-gray, Wolfe left the campsite and made his way to the wide flat rock he knew overlooked the valley below. He sat cross-legged on the rock, extended his arms to the lightening sky and began to pray to the rising sun that was beginning its journey to the waters in the west, and its daily visit with Changing Woman.

If Father Sun was listening, perhaps he would tell him what to do, Wolfe thought. About his latest problem with the Anglos. And the strange, enticing woman who'd literally fallen into his life.

Unfortunately, it had been a long time since any of the Holy Ones had told him anything useful. There were times when it seemed as if his gods had stopped listening to him because of his life in the white world.

The curved edge of the sun appeared on the eastern horizon, its bloodred color seeping across the edge of the world and turning the mountains from black to purple. Wolfe stood up, his voice rising. As he chanted aloud, his words echoed in the canyon.

His voice deepened and grew louder. It trembled with a depth of emotion that came close to fury, making it sound as if he were defying Father Sun instead of asking for his help.

And when he finally stopped chanting and his words drifted away like cottonwood down on a stiff breeze, there was nothing but lonely silence to take their place.

7

AWAKENED BY the chirping of birds, Noel felt refreshed, quiet and relaxed, as if she'd awakened from a great fever.

The pale light revealed that she'd slept through the night. When a wide wet tongue swiped a good-morning against her cheek, she laughed and hugged the big dog.

"So, you followed us here," she murmured into its shaggy yellow fur. "I hope you didn't bring anyone with you."

Her first thought, when she realized she was alone, was that Wolfe had ridden off and left her to face the posse. The sight of his mare, tethered beside Black Jack's stolen horse, was a decided relief.

A morning chill had striped the forest with bands of pale fog. The wispy swatches picked up the crimson light as the sun rose above the rim. Reluctantly leaving the warmth of the bedroll, Noel stood up, flinching as muscles still suffering the effects of her accident and the long ride, protested painfully. Ignoring the aches and pains, she took off after Wolfe, following the dog who seemed to know the way.

She heard him first. Then saw him, standing there, illuminated in the crimson light, arms and face uplifted to the bloodred sun. As he chanted the sacred words, his singsong tone curled through her, vibrating deep inside her, echoing throughout her body, like the pulsing of blood in her veins.

It was then she realized exactly how different Wolfe Longwalker was from the other men she knew. Despite his mixed blood, Wolfe was definitely a nineteenth-century Indian. A warrior. If he'd been born fifty years earlier, he would have wielded tomahawk and bows and arrows against the white intruders. Instead, he had taken up the only weapon he knew, waging a war of words against his enemies.

By the time he ceased chanting, the sun had risen over the edge of the world and the warm orange light was giving way to a blue as bright and shimmering as the distant sea.

Wolfe had, of course, been aware of her the moment she'd approached. He'd considered stopping his morning prayer, then decided that it was better that she see him as he was. Better that she knew how different their worlds were.

"You are awake," he said.

"Yes." Her smile was hesitant. "Good morning. I didn't mean to disturb you."

"Then you should have stayed wherever you came from. Where you belong." Wolfe regretted his harsh words when they caused her to flinch. But he did not apologize.

"I'm sorry," she murmured. Biting her lip, she looked away, out over the vast valley.

"That is not necessary." He closed the distance between them and looked down at her. Her slide of blond hair, lit by the rising sun, gleamed like molten silver. When the morning breeze blew a strand against her cheek, he brushed it away, ignoring the faint warning growl of the dog.

"Is the wolf sorry it has to hunt the deer? Does the bear feel sad when it eats a fish? You should not apologize for having come here." He shrugged. "It is the way things are. Sorry changes nothing."

His touch was gentle. Almost tender. But his expression remained frustratingly unreadable. "I was surprised when I woke up this morning and discovered yesterday wasn't a dream. That I really was here. With you." She sighed softly. "Sometimes it's difficult to separate truth from dreams."

It was the mention of her dream that caused recognition to come crashing down on him and Wolfe realized that this was the woman he'd dreamed about in his cell. Not prepared to share that information, he turned his mind to more mundane matters.

"Are you hungry?"

"Famished," she admitted. "I think I could eat a horse."

"Hopefully, it will not come to that."

Remembering that these were different times, she said quickly, "I was speaking figuratively."

His lips quirked suspiciously. "I know. As was I."

"Oh." Her lips curved. "Don't look now, Wolfe, but I think you almost made a joke."

Enjoying the warmth of her dazzling smile too much for comfort, he merely grunted and turned away. Leaving her once again to follow him.

It was a beautiful day. The lingering drops of morning dew on the lush greenery along the riverbank captured the sunlight, breaking it into rainbows that swirled in the blades of the grass and the bright spring leaves of the trees.

He made a pot of coffee on the still-glowing embers of the previous night's fire. Noel drank a mug of the strong dark brew and watched him restore the sharp edge of a bone-handled knife with swift strokes of the whetstone he'd taken from his saddlebag. His hands were long and dark, his movements graceful and sure.

A not uncomfortable silence settled over them and for a time, there was only the rasp of stone on metal, and the flutter of birds in the tree branches overhead.

He tested the blade with his thumb. Satisfied, he cut a pair of twigs from a nearby willow and sharpened the ends to a point.

Then, using rocks as stepping-stones, he made his way to the center of the river, where he stood, watching the fish darting in and out among the rocks, breaking the surface with a silvery flare, then vanishing with a flip of their fins.

Every muscle in his body was taut with concentration, every atom of his attention was directed down into the flowing water. Noel watched him lift the handmade spear, watched it descend on a swift stroke, then emerge with a pan-size trout. The scales of the fish glistened like quicksilver in the morning sun.

"That was wonderful," she said, not as surprised as she might have been only yesterday. Although the biography in the *Rogues Across Time* book had stressed his life spent in the white world, she realized that, having witnessed his morning prayer, he was still very much a Navajo, attuned to the land, accustomed to living with it on its terms.

"It is not so difficult." He mentally thanked the fish for giving its life then returned to the riverbank.

"I couldn't do it."

"You are not Navajo."

From his tone, Noel got the distinct impression that Wolfe was reminding her, yet again, of the differences between them. "No," she agreed mildly. "I'm not."

After cleaning the fish, he laced the fillets onto the twigs and held the slabs of pink flesh over the glowing coals until they turned white and the edges charred black. They ate the fish right off the sticks, and Noel, accustomed to the finest of European cuisine, could not remember when she'd enjoyed a meal more.

"That was delicious," she said happily.

He watched her lick her fingers and once more felt an annoying tug deep in his groin. He wanted her, dammit. He wanted to lose himself in her soft feminine warmth, wanted to kiss her mouth, her breasts, that warm honeyed place between her legs. He wanted to push her down on his bedroll and take her hard and fast, and when the ride was over, he wanted to do it again.

Which was precisely the problem, Wolfe reminded himself. One time with this woman would not be enough. He'd want more. And the wanting would make him weak. And vulnerable. Although he'd never considered himself a remotely cautious man, neither was he a fool. Making love with the princess Noel was a risk he dared not take.

"Although the idea may be difficult to accept for those who embrace the reservation system, my people were capable of feeding themselves long before they ever saw a white man."

The sun was warm, her stomach was filled, and although she knew, on some distant level, that she should be worried about the posse that was bound to be following them, not to mention concerned about her uncertain future, at the moment, Noel felt too good to get into an argument.

"Of course you were." She leaned back against the rocks and enjoyed the sight of the sun-gilded river polishing its rocks. "Paradise must look a great deal like this," she murmured as much to herself as to Wolfe.

"It is good land," he agreed. "Too good, some would say, for a bunch of damn savages."

"You're not a savage."

"That's not what the papers say. Everyone knows I massacred those settlers. Which is why they want to hang me."

"You didn't do it."

"You're so sure of that?"

"Yes." Refusing to let him intimidate her with that cold stare, she glared back at him. "I'd bet my life on it."

"Did you ever think," he suggested grimly as he stood up and walked over to where he'd tethered the horses, "that's precisely what you're doing?"

Frustrated, Noel refused to dignify the vague threat with an answer.

Instead she concentrated on her surroundings. Accustomed to her tidy, landlocked home, the vast, seemingly endless landscape they were riding through took Noel's breath away. The dramatic, towering red-sandstone sculptures made her feel as if they were crossing a mystical land born from dreams rather than reality.

"It's so open," she breathed during a brief pause for a drink of water to cut the dust. She handed back the canteen he'd refilled from the river. "It's as if we're on another planet."

He glanced around the hauntingly lonely landscape. "Sometimes, if you listen intently enough, you can hear the spirits walking."

Wolfe knew that such a remark would only add to his image as a savage. How could she understand that no matter how far he roamed, this place between the four sacred mountains would always represent *Shu'kayah*, his home. He was irrevocably bound to it—physically and emotionally.

Although anywhere else she may have found his claim of spirits unbelievably fanciful, Noel understood what he was saying perfectly. Although this may be the loneliest place on the planet, she had the feeling they were not alone. Not wanting to try to explain what she couldn't understand, herself, she continued to drink in the moving view.

"That's an interesting shape," she murmured, pointing at one tall spire standing alone in the red earth.

"That's Spider Rock. Navajos believe that it was Spider Woman who lives atop the rock, who first taught the Dineh how to weave. In the beginning, the women weavers always left a hole in the center of the blanket—"

"Like a web."

He nodded. "Exactly. Unfortunately, the white traders refused to buy these blankets, which presented a problem, because if the tribute to her is denied, Spider Woman will weave webs in the head of the weaver."

"Cobwebs in the brain," Noel murmured. "I think I've had that a few times, myself."

Wolfe smiled. "So have I."

This time, the look they exchanged was one of shared pleasure, without any sensual overtones. It crossed Wolfe's mind that as foolhardy as it was to want this woman, to actually like her and enjoy her company could ultimately prove even more dangerous.

"So what did they do?" she asked. "To satisfy Spider Woman, and still be able to sell their blankets?"

"Oh." He shrugged off the discomforting feeling. "Most weavers still leave a spirit outlet in the design." His expression hardened as he thought of all the concessions that had been made to satisfy others who could not begin to understand the complexity of his people's belief system.

His people had never wanted to make the white men like them. So why, Wolfe had asked himself again and again, did the Americans seem so anxious to change the Dineh? To make them like them. It shouldn't have to be that way, he considered. There was plenty of room for all.

But the whites had wanted more and more land. They found metals and they wanted to mine them. They found coal and they wanted to mine it. If Indians happened to be living there, the white man's solution was merely to move them somewhere else, never minding that it was their land. Their copper. Their coal.

The damn whites were like maggots on a dead coyote. Every day there were more and more maggots and less and less coyote. Until finally the day came when there was nothing left for the maggots to eat and the coyote was just bones.

"We're wasting time," he said abruptly. Kicking his mare's flanks, he began riding again.

Something had happened. The brief, easygoing mood was gone, replaced by that edgy anger she'd come to expect. Looking at his grim expression and hard eyes, Noel found him almost the model of the cruel savage his detractors wanted others to believe him to be.

Knowing better, she held her tongue yet again and continued on.

The sun was setting as they reached Canyon de Chelly, making the red sandstone glow ruby and gold. Viewed from the rim of the gorge, the green cornfields, orchards, horses and hogans on the canyon floor below seemed like a child's toys.

"It's the most spectacular thing I've ever seen." Noel was awestruck by the bird's-eye view. "Do people actually live in those?" she asked, her gaze settling on the multistoried stone dwellings tucked into alcoves on the towering cliffs. The remarkable stone buildings were, in their own way, as breathtaking as any palaces built by her European ancestors.

"Not for about seven hundred years." Once again, Wolfe found himself reluctantly enjoying the awe on her face. It matched his own feelings. A person could not live surrounded by so much living history and not feel connected to the people who had once lived between these great pink cliffs now claimed by the Dineh.

"The cliff dwellings were built by people we call the *Anasazi*," he said. "It's a Navajo word meaning the ancient ones. They lived here, in Canyon de Chelly, for about nine hundred years, until disappearing sometime in the thirteenth century."

"Where did they go?"

"There are several theories. Until the good people of Whiskey River decided to hang me, I was planning to write a book about one of the possibilities."

"You will write it," Noel said with absolute conviction. Looking down at the stone city again, she repeated the name of the canyon, pronouncing it as he had, Canyon *de shay*.

"It means, where the water comes out of the rock. Even in the driest of years, when the rest of our land is suffering drought, the springs flow in this canyon. That was, undoubtedly, the appeal to the Basketmakers, who were the first to arrive here before the birth of Christ."

"And to think that we Europeans smugly think America is a young country," she murmured.

"White European America is still in its fledgling stage. What too many historians chose to overlook is that there were indigenous people living here long before the first Pilgrim came ashore at Plymouth Rock."

And although the government had allowed his people to return to Dinetah, they were still not free. It was not right, Wolfe thought furiously, that the Dineh were unable to go wherever they wanted, to hunt, to raid or just to ride out onto the vastness of the high desert to converse with the gods. And to seek the comforting solitude that could be found beneath the wide sky.

"That's why you write your stories," she guessed. "To provide a balance to the historians."

He was uncomfortable with her understanding his motives so well. He'd learned early in life that the secret of survival was to keep everyone at arm's length, to hold them far enough away that they couldn't reach you. Couldn't touch you in the places that mattered most.

"I hate to disappoint you, Princess, but my reasons for writing are not all that noble. The truth is that my books have earned me a great deal of money and access to a world I never would have experienced if I'd stayed here in Canyon de Chelly and dedicated my life to growing corn and herding sheep."

"It may have earned you wealth. But I think you still feel like an outsider in that world."

Storm clouds moved across his face and darkened his indigo eyes. "It was once taboo to go beyond the four sacred mountains. It was believed that outside the land created by the Holy Ones, happiness is impossible."

He rubbed the back of his neck where his muscles were twisting themselves into painful knots. This was not exactly Wolfe's favorite subject. "There are also times when I feel like an outsider in my mother's world, as well," he said quietly, surprised and annoyed to hear himself admitting the secrets of his heart. "But at least I know that my clan will always be here for me."

It was something she understood. Perfectly. Her smile bloomed like the wild blue lupine beneath the soft spring mother rains. "I feel the same way about my family."

"Back in Montacroix."

She knew he still didn't quite believe her. "Yes."

He gave her another long frustrated look. Then, muttering a curse, dug his heels against his horse's flanks and began descending the twisting narrow trail to the canyon floor.

Their arrival garnered immediate attention. Dogs began a furious barking and people poured out of the beehive hogans. Children came running up to them, laughing and clapping their hands. Women, clad in velveteen blouses and full calico skirts followed, their expressions guarded as they viewed the obvious outsider Wolfe had brought into their midst. Bringing up the rear were the men. Although not as tall as Wolfe, they looked hard. Beneath the brims of their battered and sweat-stained felt Stetsons, their dark faces had been weathered to the consistency of boot leather.

Wolfe reined in his horse. "It would be best if you waited until I explain our situation."

Noel nodded her acquiescence, then watched as he dismounted and walked up to a woman she guessed to be in her mid-fifties. The mangy yellow dog waited with her.

The woman's expression was as serious as Wolfe's as they exchanged words. Twice, something he'd said caused the woman's midnight eyes to flick inscrutably over Noel, then she returned her attention to Wolfe. Finally, her broad face split into a huge smile and Noel watched the tension drain from Wolfe's tense shoulders. His answering smile was warmer and more intimate than any he'd bestowed upon her.

A man from the back of the crowd called out something. Wolfe answered, causing everyone to break into boisterous laughter. There were more questions. More answers.

And still Noel waited.

A lifetime of regal training, instilled in her from the cradle, kept her from squirming beneath the slanted looks and the comments she could not translate but knew were about her.

Finally, just when her nerves were stretched to the point of screaming, Wolfe turned toward her as if suddenly remembering her presence.

"It's not every day I bring a woman back with me from the outside," he said in explanation. And, she thought, in apology.

"Especially a white woman wearing a prostitute's red dress," she suggested mildly.

"There is that," Wolfe agreed. Although his tone was dry, rare laughter gleamed in his gaze.

"Do you come home often?" From the exuberant welcome he'd received, she suspected he was not a frequent visitor.

"Not as much as I'd like." Fame, Wolfe had discovered, had proven unreasonably time-consuming. "The last time was in February. When my brother was married."

"Your brother? I thought you were an only child."

"Being a matriarchal society, our maternal aunts are thought of as our second mothers, so we refer to the children of our mothers' sisters as our brothers and sisters."

"What about the children of your father's sisters?"

"They are thought of much as they are in your white world. As cousins. Children of a father's sister belong to his clan, while children of his brothers belong, of course, to the clan of their mother."

"Of course," she murmured, thoroughly confused.

He laughed as he helped her down from the back of the horse. "Now you know how the rest of the world feels when trying to unravel the intricacies of European royal intermarriages," he said. "Our language differentiates many more categories of relatives than white families because the Holy Ones prescribed ways of behaving toward relatives of different classes.

"As I said, what you might consider cousins, we believe to be sisters and brothers. And although familiarity is permitted during childhood, we are forbidden to marry within our own clan. Or that of our father. My clan is particularly conservative. The males are brought up to think of *all* female members of the clan as sisters."

"Gracious." She thought about that for a moment, thought about how, until reading Wolfe's book, she'd thought of Native Americans as simple people. "It's all quite complex."

"I suppose it is." He shrugged. "For an outsider."

With that single word, he'd yet again reminded her— reminded himself—that whatever grew out of this undeniable attraction they'd shared could not be permanently rooted.

Knowing that he was right, Noel nevertheless found the idea more than a little depressing.

Although his hands had encircled her waist as he'd lifted her down to the ground, Wolfe carefully avoided any further physical contact as he led her through the crowd of children, who could not have stared at her with more fascination if she'd suddenly ridden down from the sky on one of those enormous puffy white clouds and landed in their midst.

He stopped before the woman Noel guessed to be his aunt.

"Second Mother," he addressed her formally, "this is Noel Giraudeau. She is the female who shot the man who shot me."

"So much trouble." The older woman surprised Noel by answering in English. Her eyes were friendly, but immeasurably sad. She reached into a skirt pocket and took out a small stone, which she held out to Noel. "Thank you for saving my son."

"Tradition holds that First Man and First Woman decorated Tsoodzil—the mountain marking the southern border of the sacred land—with turquoise," Wolfe explained. "It is from Tsoodzil that we get our soft female rains. But when we were making the trek back to Dinetah from exile, the mountain became a symbol of our freedom. Because it was when they first saw it, our people knew they'd returned home."

Noel realized that to Wolfe's aunt, this small piece of black-veined turquoise was more than a mere blue stone. It represented a time when Wolfe had been born. It was also, she suspected, symbolic of his having achieved freedom yet again due to Noel's intervention.

"Thank you," she said gravely as she closed her fingers around the stone that seemed to be warming her hand. "I will treasure this. Always."

As the two women exchanged a long look, Noel imagined she could view pity in Wolfe's aunt's gaze, making her wonder if her unruly feelings for this man were so obvious.

They were.

Others had crowded around him and the questions began coming fast and furious. Finally, he turned to Noel.

"This could go on for a very long time. Why don't I get you settled into Second Mother's hogan? You can wait there while I talk with my clan."

"Thank you." Unaccustomed to such blazing sunshine, she was beginning to feel a little light-headed.

They walked side by side, the dog following close behind, as if unwilling to let Noel out of its sight. "Were those real coins your aunt was wearing on her blouse?"

"Yes. Most Dineh wear their wealth. It's simpler that way since we don't have a great many banks on the reservation."

Not wanting to get into an argument, Noel decided to overlook the sarcasm in his voice.

From the outside, the dome-shaped six-sided hogan resembled a colorful earthen beehive. Pausing at the door, Noel ran her fingers over a piece of turquoise, much like the one she'd been given, that had been imbedded in the mud covering.

"The Holy People built the first hogans out of turquoise, white shell, jet and abalone shell," Wolfe said. "The colors also represent the four sacred mountains."

"You wrote in the 'Sweat Bath Song' that hogans are more than a place to eat and sleep. They're a gift from the gods."

"To the Dineh, the way we live is not merely tradition, it is *the* only way to live—we call it the Beautiful Rainbow Way. The hogan is always at the center of our world. The entire community gets together to construct a hogan and when it's completed, the *ha tathli*— what you Anglos call a medicine man—performs a Blessing Way rite, asking the Holy People to make this place happy."

If he'd been expecting her to scoff, he would have been disappointed. "I think that's lovely. My home has great sentimental value to my family, but of course, it's not quite the same."

"No. It's not."

He opened the door, which always faced east, he explained, so that the rising sun was the first thing the family saw in the morning.

Noel was surprised to find the inside of the hogan quite cozy, with juniper-log walls and ceiling. Sheepskin rugs had been spread over the earthen floor; pots, baskets and other personal belongings were hung on the wall. She decided that when you moved your home and all your worldly possessions on a routine basis, you undoubtedly learned to economize.

"Usually, women are on the south side, men on the north. But since you're a distinguished guest, Second Mother has instructed me to give you this place." He gestured to a rug against the west wall facing the doorway.

"Please thank her for me." After two days in the saddle, Noel was relieved to be able to sink onto the soft rug. She was even more gratified when Wolfe handed her the leather water canteen.

"Will we be staying here long?" she asked.

"What's the matter, Princess? Are the accommodations a bit rustic for you?" As soon as he heard the words escape his mouth, Wolfe realized that he'd spoken more harshly than the circumstances warranted.

"Not at all," she said, flashing him a sweet, totally feigned smile. "Princess Di and I took a trip together last year to the Australian outback. We spent one night in the bush in flimsy tents that blew over during a dust storm."

Once again, Wolfe found himself liking the way she stood up to him. Once again, he warned himself this was not a good sign.

"I suppose Princess Di is another member of your illustrious royal family?"

"Actually, she's a friend. Who's married to the Prince of Wales. Well, technically they're married. But they live apart."

"The Prince of Wales happens to be married to Princess Alexandra of Denmark." Wolfe knew this well because when his publisher had sent him to England, Edward had insisted on taking him to all the city's nightspots.

"Prince *Edward* was married to Alexandra," Noel agreed. "But Prince *Charles* is married to Diana."

"Charles."

"Eldest son of Queen Elizabeth. Who ascended to the throne when her father, King George VI, died in 1952."

Wolfe shook his head. "I'll say this for you, Princess, once you concoct a story, you stick to it."

Before she could argue yet again, he turned on his heel and went striding out the door.

Deciding that he was angry because he thought she was still lying, Noel sighed. What she had no way of knowing was that Wolfe *was* angry—but at himself. Because, as she'd looked up at him, with that absolute surety of conviction gleaming in her calm blue eyes, he'd been all too tempted to kiss her. Which, while she was an honored guest in his family's hogan, would be taboo.

He rejoined the others in a nearby communal hogan, and told the story of his arrest and incarceration. There was a long drawn-out silence after Wolfe related his tale as everyone considered the implications of what they'd just heard.

"There is only one solution," a gray-haired, much-respected elder said finally.

"What is that?"

"We must have an Enemy Way performed for you."

Wolfe decided that the fact that he'd been expecting a suggestion that he leave now, before he drew the white posse and bounty hunters into Canyon de Chelly, suggested he'd been too long among the white people. Loyalties among the Dineh ran as deep and constant as the underground springs in this canyon.

"I cannot risk staying here for nine days," he argued. "It is too dangerous for you."

There had not been an organized campaign of white violence against his people since the treaty of 1868, the treaty that allowed them to return to Dinetah. But Wolfe knew that were he to remain hiding out here in the canyon, he would give those men who believed that the only good red man was a dead red man an excuse to slaughter his people.

This he could not allow.

"It is dangerous for you to walk among the whites," another older man, the brother of his mother's sister's husband observed what Wolfe had already discovered the hard way.

"You belong here," a third voice chimed in.

"We will fight to protect you," a fourth insisted. The young man jumped to his feet and held a hunting rifle over his head.

"There will be no fighting," Wolfe insisted. "Not here. Which is why I must leave."

"You cannot leave without an Enemy Way," the first man said, bringing the conversation back to the starting point. "Unless you rid your body of the sickness from being tainted by the enemy, you will die without bullets."

There was a murmur of agreement.

"Perhaps we can come up with a compromise," a quiet voice said from the back of the hogan.

Wolfe recognized the voice immediately. Many Horses's merry smile had proven a soothing source of comfort during those long lonely nights at the Eastern boarding school they'd been forced to attend.

"A compromise would be appreciated, my friend."

The man Wolfe had loved like a brother smiled, his solemn dark eyes exchanging similar boyhood memories. "I have been studying the Blackening Way with Red Hawk," he said, naming another healer.

"This is only a shortened version of the Enemy Way. It is not as effective." The older man bristled, clearly not happy about losing a potential patient. Especially to a mere upstart.

Despite Wolfe's white education, a deep primal part of him clung to old beliefs. "How long would it take?"

His childhood friend's expression had turned as solemn as Wolfe's own. "A day and a night. You could go alone into the Canyon del Muerto and fast tonight in preparation. We could begin tomorrow morning at dawn."

"That is not long enough," the detractor complained. "There has been much contamination. Only an Enemy Way will drive away the evil."

A day and a night. Long enough for the men following them to reach the canyon, Wolfe feared.

"We will take care of any *bilaganna* who wish to hurt you," someone suggested. The unflattering term was the Dineh word for white.

Wolfe's head spun and he impaled the young man who'd waved his rifle with a sharp warning glare. "There is to be no killing."

"Of course not. But we can sure slow them down," the man said.

There was a united burst of laughter that seemed to have the effect of releasing the tension from the room.

Deciding to risk the delay, Wolfe sat back and listened as his lifelong friend described the Blackening Way.

8

"YOU'RE GOING to do what?" Noel stared at Wolfe in disbelief.

"A Blackening Way. It's a shortened version of the Enemy Way."

"So you said."

After changing into more practical clothes contributed by Wolfe's aunt, she'd accompanied him away from the gathering of hogans to a private place where his clan's corn was planted beside a stream. They were sitting on a wide flat boulder overlooking the water. The yellow dog lay at their feet happily basking in the sun.

"And this is supposed to drive out whatever evils resulted in your contamination with white people. With those you call *bilaganna*."

"Just my enemies," he corrected. "Not all white people." Because he wanted to reach out and smooth away the frown lines from her forehead, he closed his hands into a fist. "Not you."

"Isn't that a relief." Her tone was thick with sarcasm, but she could not hide the relief that flooded into her eyes.

Wolfe felt an uncharacteristic need to try to explain his feelings regarding the ceremony. "When I was sent back East to the white boarding school, I would look at all the cities the train was passing through on the journey and see how all those Anglos lived so closely together. I would wonder how one old and bearded man could possibly hear the prayers of so many white people."

"Faith is accepting without understanding," Noel murmured.

"Yes." He nodded gravely. If they agreed on nothing else concerning what he was about to do, they could agree on this. "The Blackening Way is to restore *hozho*, the balance between harmony and peace."

"And restore you to the Beautiful Rainbow Way."

He searched her expression for disbelief or scorn and found neither. "Exactly."

There was a long silence, the only sound that of the tasseled green corn rustling softly in the breeze.

"Well, then." She let out a deep breath. "I think you should do it."

Although he hadn't brought her here to ask her advice, her willingness to accept a belief so alien to her own pleased him.

He was lowering his head, intent on kissing her, when an image suddenly swirled in her mind, causing her to gasp.

He pulled back. "What's wrong?"

"It's nothing." Her throat had gone as dry as the red dust beneath her feet. She swallowed.

"You have gone as pale as *Sisnajini*." Concerned, he ran the back of his hand down her white cheeks.

His gentle touch did nothing to restore calm. "*Sisnajini?*" she repeated on a ragged whisper easily heard in this vastly quiet place.

"The eastern mountain, the source of the male rains. First Man and First Woman decorated it with white shells and fastened it to the ground with white lightning. Your complexion reminds me of those shells."

As impossible as it seemed, the story no longer seemed mere myth. Because of what she had seen.

"I saw you." She began to tremble. "You were standing on a bent rainbow, dressed all in black, and this horrible giant was throwing spears at you, which were really lightning bolts." She closed her eyes. "And then there was blood. So much blood."

He might still question her story about time travel but Wolfe no longer disbelieved her claim of special vision. "That's the giant Yei Tsoh," he said quietly. "He devoured our people at the beginning of the world. It looked as if we would die out. Until the hero twins killed him and cut off his head."

She opened her eyes, her gaze shadowed with fear and dread. "You're going to fight this giant, Yei Tsoh."

"It's only a ritual battle," he assured her.

"No." The single word came out on a soft, unsteady breath. "It's much more than that." She placed her hand on his arm as her eyes pleaded with him. "It's dangerous. This Blackening Way could turn out to be more fatal to you than those men who are following us."

"It will be all right." Wolfe wished that he felt as confident as he sounded. "*I* will be all right."

A few tears escaped her worried blue eyes; Wolfe brushed them away with his fingertip. "You've obviously inherited your grandmother's gift of second sight. Do you look like her, as well?"

Noel watched the subtle change in his eyes and tried to remind herself that she hadn't come all this way to get emotionally or romantically involved with an outlaw. She was, after all, an engaged woman.

"Not at all." When she felt herself beginning to drown in those warm indigo depths, Noel dragged her gaze away and tried desperately to picture Bertran's pleasant, unthreatening face. When she couldn't envision her fiancé, her nerves tangled even more painfully. "Katia was everyone's fantasy of queen of the Gypsies."

Although her mind could not conjure up Bertran's image, she had no trouble at all remembering the life-size portrait of her grandmother as a young woman, hanging in the palace back home.

Clad in a traditional scarlet flamenco dress trimmed with an ebony lace flounce, Katia's dark hair had been a wild, unruly tangle around her shoulders, and her eyes—more black than brown—had flashed with tempestuous fire.

"My sister is the one in the family who resembles her most. Physically and emotionally." Her lips curved in a faint smile at the memory of some of Chantal's more outrageous antics over the years. "Caine always says that the first time he saw Chantal, he thought he heard the clatter of castanets and smelled the smoke from Gypsy campfires."

From her tone, Wolfe suspected Noel was actually unaware of her own stunning beauty. "She sounds quite glamorous."

"She's spectacular." Noel's smile displayed not the slightest jealousy of her sister. To resent Chantal's natural flamboyance would be like blaming the blazing golden sun for eclipsing the softer, paler light of the moon. "Before she settled down to marriage and children, newspaper columnists all over America called her the quintessential fairy-tale princess."

"And what do those newspaper writers call you?"

"I don't make the society columns all that much," she hedged, pretending a sudden interest in smoothing out the wrinkles in the full skirt she was wearing. "After all,

I'm a great deal more low-key than Chantal or Burke, and I prefer to keep in the background, doing my work and—"

She'd begun to talk too much and too fast again. Wolfe wondered if she realized how delightful she was when flustered. "What do they call you?" he repeated.

His quiet, unyielding tone drew her reluctant attention back to him. "The ice princess."

When she'd been younger, in her teens, the tag had hurt. These days, although she'd grown used to it, understood that the paparazzi had chosen it merely to accentuate the vast differences between the two royal sisters, there were occasions, such as now, when it stung.

Although he knew that he was venturing into quicksand, Wolfe was unable to ignore such an obvious challenge. "I always knew that newspaper writers were idiots."

As she dragged her nervous fingers through the silk slide of her hair, he reached out and captured her hand, linking their fingers together. "You're much too warm-blooded for anyone to think of you as glacial, Princess."

To prove his point, he brushed his lips across her knuckles, satisfied by the sharp intake of breath. "Too responsive."

Her mouth had gone as dry as the arid red land they'd spent the past day riding across. She swallowed, resisting the urge to snatch her hand away, knowing it would only let him know how strongly his touch affected her.

"Too passionate."

When his teeth nipped at the fleshy part of her hand, Noel decided that it was time—past time—to make him understand she had not come all this way to tumble into his bedroll.

"You shouldn't say such things," she insisted on a voice she wished was stronger. More authoritative.

Wolfe's answering smile was slow. Wicked. Deliberate. "Too late."

There was a moment, just before his mouth touched hers, when the intensity in his dark eyes warned Noel that Wolfe Longwalker was a very dangerous man. And if she didn't back away now while she still could, she'd be making a very big mistake.

But then he was kissing her and she forgot to think at all.

Unlike that first time, upstairs in the Road to Ruin, his mouth didn't crush her's. Nor did it plunder.

Instead, with a touch as soft as dandelion fluff, as benevolent as summer sunshine, his lips brushed over hers without lingering, leaving warmth from one corner to the other, inviting her into the mists. Murmuring his name as she framed his ruggedly handsome face with her hands, she went willingly.

It was as if he intended to kiss her endlessly. There were no demands. There was no rush. There were only shimmering sighs, soft murmurs and a glorious golden pleasure that seeped into her bloodstream. A soft breeze whispered across her face, but his breath was so much warmer. Her head began to swim as his strong sure hands moved through her hair. Her body turned fluid, her muscles went lax.

Without surrendering the gentleness, without passion or fire, he took the kiss deeper. Then deeper still, drawing a trembling breath from her that shuddered into his mouth.

Her lips were as sweet as honey, as potent as whiskey. Even as they turned more urgent beneath his, even as her murmurs became moans, even as the way she began to arch her warm, feminine body against his caused his need to claw at him, Wolfe refused to hurry, forcing himself to keep the pace achingly slow, teasing them both.

As the sun rose higher overhead, Wolfe continued to battle hunger, fight back greed. With a patience he'd never known he possessed, he took Noel places she'd never been, gave her a glimpse of a world unlike any she'd ever imagined.

But even his iron control had its limits. It was impossible, with her body melting against his—in total surrender, total trust—not to ache. It was futile, as her graceful hands skimmed up and down his back, not to burn.

When Wolfe felt the passion begin to burn through his loins, when he began to imagine stripping away the borrowed clothes from her lissome body, then taking her quickly, while the birds sang in the nearby fruit trees and the wind whistled in the corn and the stream flowed over polished red rocks on its way to the sea, he buried his face in her hair and took a deep breath.

She heard him say her name. *Noel.* It was like a promise. A prayer. And then, another word, which she could not translate, but recognized all too well to be a curse.

"That should not have happened." His voice, while not as strong as usual, was both flat and final. And, she thought miserably, heavy with self-disgust.

Wanting—needing—to hold on to the delicious, drugging heaviness a bit longer, she hesitated before opening her eyes. When she did, she found herself staring into a gaze so intense, she wondered if Wolfe could see all the way into her heart.

Noel had never been one to lie. Not even to herself. Especially to herself. That being the case, she was not about to begin now.

"I think it was inevitable," she suggested softly. "From the beginning."

He shook his head. "I took advantage of your confusion. And your fear."

"I may have been confused, Wolfe, but believe me, a woman, no matter what century she lives in, knows when she wants to be kissed."

"And you wanted to be kissed."

She met his probing look with a level gaze of her own. "Absolutely."

Reminding herself that discretion was the better part of valor, she did not add that by the time he'd broken off that heady kiss, she'd wanted more. Much, much more.

Even as he felt his body cooling, Wolfe's gaze drifted to her lips and felt another deep painful tug of hunger. He took both her hands in his, lacing their fingers together.

"You are an extremely passionate woman, Princess Noel de Montacroix," he assured her. "And I enjoy kissing you." He watched the warm memories of that kiss flood into her remarkable eyes and realized that although they were so far apart on so many things, about this they were in total accord. "Very much."

His thumb gently brushed across her knuckle. "Too much, perhaps."

It was happening all over again. Noel felt herself being pulled into the warmth of his masculine gaze, and wondered if part of this unruly attraction was due to the dangerous dramatic circumstances in which they'd met. Danger, she reminded herself, thinking back on Belle's words, was a powerful aphrodisiac.

Perhaps, if their paths had crossed in some ordinary, everyday way—either in his time or her's—they would have merely shared some pleasant conversation, a bit of congenial companionship.

"It's our situation," she said, wondering who she was trying to convince. Herself? Or him? "It's bound to heighten emotions." The practical side of her, the side that had always ruled her behavior—and her heart—felt much better now that she'd solved the problem.

Wolfe considered that possibility and instantly dismissed it. However, since it was more than a little obvious that it was important to Noel that she believe her analysis of the shared desire that had sparked between them from the beginning, he decided there was no point in distressing her further by arguing.

"I suppose that's a possibility," he mused out loud, resisting the urge to capture those rosy lips again and kiss her senseless.

"It's the only answer," she said firmly.

That's all it was, she assured herself as they returned to the hogan. It was all she could allow it to be.

NAKED, save for a deerskin breechcloth favored by his ancestors, before the invading Spanish and *bilagaana* had introduced shirts and trousers to his people, Wolfe galloped along the floor of the canyon, enjoying the feel of the sun beating down on his bare back and the wind rushing against his face. The mare strained for speed beneath him, her hooves kicking up clouds of red dust as he urged her on.

Behind him he heard the pounding of other hooves. Without taking time to look over his shoulder, Wolfe dug his heels into the mare's flanks and pushed her harder. Faster. Trying to outrun his pursuer. Trying to outrun his torment. And most of all, trying to outrun his princess-hunger.

The latter, he feared, would be impossible.

Finally, taking pity on his stouthearted mare, Wolfe reined in. Moments later, his childhood friend caught up with him.

"One of these days, I'll beat you," the moon-faced man said, cheerful in his acknowledgment of Wolfe's victory.

"In the North, perhaps," Wolfe said, referring to the Navajo afterworld. "But not before."

"Probably not," Many Horses said with a resigned sigh. "You have always been the best rider in both our clans. And the best storyteller."

"And you have always been good to my clan." Wolfe knew he owed a tremendous debt of gratitude to this man, who in so many ways was like a brother to him and who saw to so many of his aunt's immediate needs. "Taking care of so many of my responsibilities while I spend too much time away in the white world."

"You would not have become so wealthy if you'd remained here in Dinetah."

Wolfe's curse was short and crude.

"And," the man continued, "if you had not become wealthy, your clan would not have nearly so many sheep. Last winter, when so many people lost livestock in the blizzards, those sheep, bought with the money you so generously sent home, kept *all* our people alive. Not just the Bitter Water Clan."

"That's me," Wolfe muttered. "Savior to the Dineh."

"You have been called worse."

Wolfe laughed at that as he was supposed to. Then felt himself relaxing for the first time since his arrest.

"There are many who were surprised that you would bring an Anglo female here," Many Horses said carefully as they walked their horses back to camp.

"I didn't have any choice. She killed a man trying to help me escape. I couldn't leave her for the hangman."

"It would be a shame for such a pretty neck to be stretched." Many Horses grinned. "At least, if you are captured, you will have spent your last days pleasurably... Several men back in Whiskey River would probably like to hang you just for taking the blond whore away from her brothel."

"She's not a whore." Wolfe's jaw clenched. His eyes hardened.

"She dresses like one."

"That's a long story."

"I see." His longtime friend gave him a long, considering look. "You care for this woman." It was not a question.

"Any man would be grateful to someone for trying to save his life," Wolfe muttered.

"True. But I think it is more than that." There was another pause. "I think you want her."

"What man wouldn't?"

"I think you want her for more than a warm moist place to plant your seed. I think you want her for a wife."

"You're wrong," Wolfe answered quickly. Too quickly, he realized as his friend's gaze narrowed. "She's Anglo."

"So was your father."

"That was different. My father raped my mother. For that reason alone he should have died."

A muscle clenched in Wolfe's jaw as he thought about how many times over the years he'd considered killing the soldier responsible for his mother's tragic fate. But he'd never been able to learn the man's identity.

"I think," Many Horses said with a bold, masculine wink, "you would not have to rape this Anglo woman. The way she looks at you, making love to you with her eyes, tells me that she would willingly spread her legs for the famous Wolfe Longwalker."

"She's promised to another."

"Promises have been broken." He flashed another quick grin. "If they have taught us nothing else, the white men have shown us that their promises change like the moon. It is obvious that she wants you, Wolfe. Not many men could turn down the opportunity to bed such a woman."

It was the same thing Wolfe had been telling himself. The problem was, he had the feeling that the princess with the corn-silk hair was not a woman whose bed a man could easily walk away from.

And that, he reminded himself, was the reason he would continue to resist temptation. No matter how appealing.

As he entered the ceremonial hogan, Wolfe knew that it was important—imperative—that he banish his princess from his thoughts before his upcoming confrontation with the monster Yei Tsoh.

Aided by Many Horses, he washed himself with water mixed with medicinal herbs. After this ceremonial washing, he lifted the bowl and drank the remaining water.

His mind was fully focused as he took his place on the woolen rug that had been spread on the dirt floor. In the center of the rug, woven by Second Mother, were the four sacred plants of the Dineh—corn, squash, beans and tobacco. Guarding the eastern edge of the rug—the only side not protected by the Rainbow, was the woven image of a medicine bundle.

The healer, Red Hawk, had already taken his place at the hogan's western wall and was singing a song to call the deities from the four sacred mountains.

Wolfe knew that Red Hawk could see things they could not see, and knew things they would never know. Like all such holy men, he was custodian of the past and intermediary to the world beyond. He could talk to the gods, talk to the animals, and the clouds. And unlike the silence Wolfe had heard far too often in his life, they would answer Red Hawk.

Many Horses's usually merry expression was grave as he picked up a bowl of thick mutton tallow and proceeded to spread it over Wolfe's naked body.

A chill of expectation mixed with foreboding went through Wolfe. Although the side of him that had been educated by the *bilagaanas* and that had lived and worked in their world assured him he had nothing to fear, and despite those reassuring words he'd spoken to Noel, another deeper, primal part of his subconscious worried that he might not survive the upcoming battle alive.

The singing continued, a steady, droning chant. Smoke rose from the fire, rising to the open hole in the domed roof of the hogan. Beneath the thick coating of tallow, Wolfe began to sweat.

"And now don your armor." Reaching into a bowl, Many Horses took out a handful of ash made from a juniper tree that had been struck by lightning. "The armor that the Holy Twins wore to defeat the giants. The armor that will make you invisible to the giants."

He spread the grainy mixture over Wolfe, giving him the appearance that had earned the ceremony the name, Blackening Way.

As the medicine man continued to sing, Many Horses tied wristbands braided from strips of yucca around Wolfe's wrists. More strips had been tied together, meant to be worn over the body, serving as additional armor against the deadly enemy. As the medicine man chanted about Wolfe's life among the *bilagaanas,* of his birth on the Long Walk, of his success in the white man's world, a success that had resulted in the white man's jealousy and hatred, the bands absorbed more and more of the infection contracted from the enemy.

Wolfe's head began to spin dizzily from the herbs that had been in the water he'd drunk. And from others that had been thrown into the fire. From the battle taking place within his body. His mind. And his heart. Sweat beaded on his darkened forehead, his upper lip, beneath his arms, running down his sides, leaving wet trails in the blackened ash.

"Step into the shoes of Monster Slayer," the medicine man sang tonelessly. "Step into the shoes of him whose lure is the extended bow string. Step into the shoes of him who lures the enemy to death."

The chant was pounding in Wolfe's ears like a leather-covered drum while lightning flashed before his eyes. Corn pollen was sprinkled over the ash clinging to his body. The yellow dust would help make him invisible to the giant.

"I am hungry," a thunderous voice boomed from somewhere above his head, echoing off the juniper walls of the hogan. Wolfe knew the voice belonged to the giant Yei Tsoh. "I will eat a Dineh tonight."

"You will soon throw those words back into Yei Tsoh's ugly mouth," Many Horses assured Wolfe as he reached into a leather medicine bundle and took out a crow's beak.

He pressed the beak, known for its healing properties, to Wolfe's feet, then began working his way up Wolfe's legs, knees, chest, back and finally his head. That act completed, he gestured upward toward the open smoke-hole, the sacred motion designed to extract the enemy's taint from the patient.

When Red Hawk instructed Wolfe to leave the hogan, in order to motion, four times in succession, away from his body and toward the sun, Wolfe discovered that his legs had turned unreasonably wobbly. He was staggering like a drunk and having a difficult time focusing. The holy place of Dinetah had become a soft-hazed world alive with the buzz of insects, and brightened by dancing lights and swirling suns.

There were more songs. More chants. All day and all night, Wolfe relived the mythical battle between his Dineh ancestors, the children of the Sun, and that fiercest of all—the alien, man-eating god.

With a mighty roar, Yei Tsoh clawed him, slicing open Wolfe's arm from shoulder to elbow. Blood gushed forth from the torn artery, flowing over the land like a river. Just when he thought he'd lost the battle, that he was going to die, a silver-edged cloud floated down from the storm-tossed sky, and out of the cloud stepped a female with hair the color of moonlight.

She was carrying a pot of magic herbs. With soothing words and a calming touch, she tended to him, bathing his wounds with empathetic tears before rubbing the herbs into the cleansed flesh.

Healed, he returned to battle. A battle that raged inside him. Around him. Battering at his senses, raging through his blood. Ripping him apart from the inside out.

Then, finally, Yei Tsoh's massive body was pierced by a chain-lightning arrow hurled at him by this new Monster Slayer, Wolfe Longwalker. As he roared in pain and fury, another arrow struck its mark, scattering shells from the giant's armor. Yei Tsoh crumpled to his knees and was staring at Wolfe in fury and disbelief as a third, and fatal arrow hit the center of his heart. He fell onto his face with a force that made the world tremble. And then, he lay still.

There were shouts of victory from the observers in the hogan. A victorious Wolfe was helped into his buckskin breechcloth and led outside the hogan, where a man wearing a Yei mask and carrying a ceremonial staff and leather shield bordered by snowy-tipped eagle feathers, was waiting with Wolfe's mare. Both man and mare were bathed in a blinding golden light from the morning sun.

Refusing Many Horses's assistance, Wolfe managed to pull himself astride the mare, and together, the men rode up the steep trail to a jutting red mesa overlooking the canyon. From this location, Whiskey River was many miles to the south.

They sat on the ground, facing east, into the rising Father Sun as Red Hawk led Wolfe through one final prayer from the Blessing Way, designed to invoke good luck, good health, and take the evil enemy away, back across the vast red landscape, back to its origins in Whiskey River.

"Hohzho naa haas glih," the singer concluded the traditional prayer. "In beauty, it is done."

With that cue, Many Horses, Wolfe and the spear carrier sprinkled corn pollen over the edge of the cliff, where the western wind caught it and carried it out over the mesa.

Although his situation had not changed, as he watched the yellow dust ride the breeze, Wolfe felt blessedly at peace.

FOR THE SECOND NIGHT in a row, Noel tossed and turned, her mind filled with bloody, horrific warlike images too terrible to contemplate. At least once an hour she'd be jerked out of her restless sleep, surprised to find herself still in Wolfe's family's hogan.

Inside, the others' breathing was soft and slow and steady. Outside, the branches of the juniper and olive trees rustled softly in the wind. Every so often, a lamb would bleat, no doubt crying out for its mother. But mostly, there was only silence. Dark, lonely, disquieting silence.

And Noel's unceasing concern for a man she feared she was, against every vestige of common sense, falling hopelessly in love with.

Giving up on sleep, she retrieved her bag from a peg on the log wall and slipped quietly out of the hogan, making her way by moonlight back down to that peaceful spot beside the stream, accompanied, as usual, by the dog.

Her nerves felt as if they were on fire, images filled her mind like billowing smoke from a fire, images of Wolfe, caught in a desperate life-or-death struggle, images of armor-clad giants, biting heads off Navajo children, images of Wolfe as she'd first seen him in her vision, bare-chested, noble, astride his horse, accepting death not with honor, but scorn.

The problem, she considered grimly, was that try as she might, she could not see Wolfe saved, living a safe and happy life. Not with the members of his clan. Not with her.

"I'm so worried about him," she told the dog, who responded by wagging his tail.

Noel knew that the idea of giants eating children were as fanciful and illogical as those tales of trolls living in her own Montacroix forests. And if there was one word that anyone who knew her would use to describe Princess Noel de Montacroix, it would be *logical*.

"The problem is," she explained to the dog, who'd now tilted his head and pricked his ears forward as if listening to her concerns, "even before Sabrina gave me that invitation that set all this in motion, even before I found that book about Wolfe in the Road to Ruin, my own experience has taught me that some things can't be explained away by logic."

Her clairvoyance, for one, she thought. And now, this adventure through time.

After Wolfe had left her at the hogan and gone off to prepare for the ceremony, she'd tried to convince herself, one last time, that this was all just a dream, triggered by the woodcut on the invitation, the *Rogues Across Time* book and Wolfe Longwalker's own Native American stories.

Any time now, she'd wake up to the aroma of Audrey Bradshaw's rich dark coffee and crumbly blueberry muffins drifting up the stairs of the bed and breakfast. And she'd telephone Chantal in Washington and together they would laugh over the dream that had seemed so real.

The dream that Noel knew was no dream at all.
She sighed.

And then, beneath the cottonwood tree, in the same place where Wolfe had kissed her to distraction, Noel sank to her knees and began to pray.

The dawn was painting the sky with brilliant fingers of scarlet and gold when Noel reluctantly decided it was time to return to the village. Her gaze drifted toward a side canyon, where Wolfe had told her the ceremonial hogan was located.

All she could see was a faint puff of gray smoke rising into the unbelievably blue sky. But a feeling of dread continued to be draped over her like a wet and heavy cloak.

She reached for her bag and felt the familiar tingling in her fingertips. Drawn by a pull she'd felt too many times in the past to ignore, she retrieved the invitation.

As she watched, the woodcut image of the burning cabin disintegrated, replaced by a scene of a muddy road lined with frame buildings. One of the frame buildings had a sign nailed above the door: The Irish Rose.

As if in a dream, she felt herself entering the building, passing through the front parlor to the stairway, then up the red-carpeted stairs and down the hall to a room that was furnished a great deal like the bedroom in Belle's Road to Ruin bordello. A man with a handlebar mustache was lying on his back on the bed, drinking whiskey out of a bottle, while a fat redheaded whore straddled his bare thighs.

Although she'd never seen a photograph of the man, Noel knew she was looking at Bret Starr. Excited, and knowing that she'd just been given an important clue, Noel nearly screamed as the vision faded away. Scooping up her bag, she ran back to the hogan to await Wolfe's return.

The village had awakened during her absence. Outside several of the hogans she passed, people were sprinkling pollen to welcome the return of the sun.

In front of one hogan, a man was slaughtering a sheep hanging from a pole while his wife sat at her loom, creating a rug much like the one Noel had seen hanging on the wall in the lobby of the bed and breakfast.

Some children were playing, shooting small arrows with their tiny blunt-tipped bows, stalking one another. Noel realized that there had been a time when such play would have been meaningful, a prelude to the intense training they would have received when they were old enough to learn the ways of the warrior. Now, it was merely the last remnant of a history that was coming to an end, just as the absolute freedom of the people who had made that history had come to an end.

The thought saddened her terribly.

Outside the hogan where she'd spent such a restless night, Second Mother sat on a wooden bench, winding red clay into a coil. Nearby, a drying pot hung from the branch of a cottonwood tree.

"May I watch?" Noel asked, not wanting to disturb the woman's creative mood.

"Of course." The walnut-dark face wreathed in a smile. "I am not one of those who believes that I must isolate myself to make a perfect pot."

"Did you make the ones inside the hogan?"

"Yes." The fingers, gnarled with age and arthritis, deftly worked the clay with a grace and skill that Noel admired. She wished that Chantal could see some of the exquisite works of art being created in this isolated nineteenth-century village.

"They're quite beautiful. My sister is an artist. She paints. Having no talent myself, I envy hers, even as I'm in awe of it."

"You have simply not found your gift," Second Mother assured her. "The Holy People determine which talents we are all to be given. See over there? Where Running Girl is weaving her rug?"

Noel nodded.

"When she was a little girl, during her vacations from boarding school, she would sit with me while I worked my clay, always begging me to teach her how to make pots. It seemed that she wanted to make pots more than anything else in the world. But the pots did not want her.

"Clay has a soul of its own. Its own song. And prayer. I taught her the songs I sing when I make my pots. She tried very hard, mixing the clay just as I taught her, singing the songs, but whenever her pots were baked, they broke. Every one."

"That must have been horribly discouraging."

"She became very sad. I told her that she was trying too hard. That she must be patient and wait for the Holy Ones to choose her gift. And eventually, Spider Woman did give her the blessing of weaving. But while Running Girl was waiting, she would not listen to me." The older woman slanted a faint smile Noel's way. "You know the stone mind of young people."

"I've been called hardheaded a few times," Noel agreed with an answering smile.

"Of course you have. Wolfe is stubborn. Like a goat. As was his mother, my sister." A fond, faraway look drifted into the coffee-brown eyes. "My sister was a basket weaver."

"Tell me about Wolfe's mother."

The soft reminiscent smile turned into a frown. "It is taboo to speak of the dead. I should not have mentioned the basket weaving. Such talk brings witches."

With that door effectively shut, Noel tried another. She took a deep breath and asked, "What about his father?"

The hands that had been patting the clay stilled. Dark eyes drifted over the landscape, but Noel had the feeling that it was not the sheep and hogans the older woman was seeing, but something else. Something from another place. Another time.

"Some people believe you are a witch, come here to bring harm to my sister's son."

"What do you think?"

Second Mother gave her a long look that, as impossible as it seemed, went all the way through Noel, all the way to her heart. And her soul. And her mind.

"I have seen my own death," the woman finally answered. Although to some, such an answer may have seemed off the point, Noel grasped her meaning immediately.

"I once saw a threat against my sister," Noel revealed. "And another against my brother. But I seem to be mostly blind regarding my own life."

Second Mother nodded, satisfied. "It happens that way, sometimes." She treated Noel to another of those knowing gazes. "You saw my son in a vision. In danger."

"Yes." Noel dipped her head. "I did. And although I don't understand it, myself, I knew that it was my destiny to come here to Arizona Territory and save him."

"You succeeded in your destiny, then."

"But not permanently. Because men are still after him. Men who are lying about what they say he's done. Men who want to kill him because he tells the truth."

"Words are powerful," Second Mother agreed. "Wolfe's words are especially powerful because they take the truth of the Dineh out to the world. Something Anglos do not want."

"Some Anglos," Noel corrected mildly.

Despite the seriousness of the subject, Second Mother's lips quirked in a vague smile. "Some Anglos," she conceded. She fell silent again, thinking quietly. "Would it help you save my son if you had a powerful Anglo man speak for him?"

Noel's instincts were humming. "It certainly couldn't hurt."

Second Mother rose from the bench and went into the hogan. Noel waited, hearing the thump, thump, thump of the shuttle as she watched Running Girl weaving nearby.

When Second Mother came out of the hogan again, she was carrying an envelope. "This was sent from Fort Prescott," she said. "To my sister many years ago. Wolfe had not yet lived one winter. But he was being raised in the way of the Dineh, so I sent back word that she had perished on the way back to Dinetah."

As Noel took the envelope, a jolt of electricity shot through her fingers. It was so strong that both women jumped back. The envelope fluttered to the ground, yellowed ivory against the red dirt.

Noel bent down and gingerly picked it up. Although the ink was faded, she could read the bold scrawl. "It's from his father? The cavalry officer who raped her?"

"He did not rape my sister." Second mother sighed and looked away again. "He loved her. And she loved him. But times were difficult and the Anglos were much-hated. As were any Dineh women who lowered themselves to sleep with the soldiers. So, my sister hid from everyone the fact that she was with child.

"Everyone but the baby's father, who, of course, recognized the changes in her body. It was only when she gave birth on the Long Walk that her secret was revealed to our people."

"So, when he wrote asking about Wolfe's mother, and his child, you told him they'd both died."

"It was better for him to think that."

Although the letter had been written years ago, the emotional state of the writer lingered like a fiery aura. Wolfe's mother had not only loved her young officer, she'd been loved in return. By a power so forceful that only death could have kept them apart.

"The same way it was better for Wolfe to be eaten up by hatred all his life? Thinking some *bilaganna* soldier raped his mother and was responsible for her death?"

"You do not understand."

"I'm sorry." Noel took a deep breath and let it out slowly, striving for calm. It was not her place to attack the woman who'd only been trying to do her best for her dead sister's son.

"Wolfe's father is an important man now," Second mother revealed. "He is a federal judge in Flagstaff. Perhaps he can help his son."

"Perhaps." Noel ran her hands along the top of the envelope, considering her options. "Thank you," she said. "And I'm sorry I was impolite."

"That is not so surprising."

"Because I'm Anglo?"

"No. Because you love my son."

Noel knew she could no longer deny it. To herself. Or to this woman who saw so much. "It's that obvious?"

"Of course." At the sound of the hooves hitting turn, Second Mother and Noel both turned toward the rider who was trotting into camp.

Noel's heart soared when she recognized, beneath the coating of black ash, this man who was so clearly her destiny. Then, mindless of what anyone would think, she went running toward him.

9

THE SIGHT OF HER, running toward him, a wide, welcoming smile on her exquisite face, shouldn't give him so much pleasure, Wolfe told himself. It shouldn't make him feel the same way he felt whenever he glimpsed the red cliffs of Canyon de Chelly. It shouldn't make him feel as if he'd come home.

But it did. He reined in his horse.

"You're back!" Relief shimmered in her wide blue eyes, echoed in her tone. The bright dawn light revealed dark smudges beneath those incredible eyes, silent testimony that her night had been as sleepless as his.

"I told you I would return," he reminded her. Without taking his gaze from her face, that pale exquisite face, he reached a hand down and patted the massive yellow head of the dog as it jumped up and down in canine welcome. The pony, accustomed to the ubiquitous dogs at the canyon, remained calm.

"I know." She drank in the sight of him, as if to convince herself that he was truly here. That he was not some vision conjured up by her desperately hopeful mind.

He was covered in black ash. Yellow pollen clung to his hair and the pungent aroma of smoke surrounded him. Noel found him wonderful.

"I was so worried. I saw things. Terrible things. You were battling with a horrid giant. I was afraid he'd eat you. But just when I was certain I would lose you for good, you killed him. With three arrows. The final one struck him in the heart."

Wolfe knew that the odds of her knowing the details of the Blackening Way were slim to none. "You were in my mind."

Her gaze turned solemn. "I have been. From the beginning."

A memory flashed in his mind. A memory of the female with hair the color of moonlight, who'd soothed his wounds with magic herbs, allowing him to return to vanquish the giant.

Wolfe was not prepared to admit to Noel's presence in the holy ceremony, since he wasn't sure what such thoughts meant.

"There's something else," she said. "This morning, I couldn't sleep, so I went for a walk. Down to where you showed me your family had planted their corn. Where you kissed me. I was sitting there, worrying about you, when I saw Bret Starr."

"In a vision." He no longer questioned her abilities.

"Yes. He was lying in bed, with a woman. The sign above the door of the building said, The Irish Rose." She frowned. "But I can't see where it is."

"The Irish Rose is in Silverton. In Colorado." Wolfe attempted to rein in the blatant hope on her face. "But even if Starr is there, we don't know that he witnessed the massacre."

"But the woodcut—"

"And even if he did," Wolfe cut her off with a swift wave of his hand, "the fact that he took off to Silverton doesn't suggest a willingness to help keep my head out of the hangman's noose."

"Then we'll just have to talk him into cooperating," Noel decided. The fact that she and Wolfe had shared, telepathically, his encounter with Yei Tsoh, had only deepened her belief that this man—and this mission—was her destiny.

"We?"

Her enthusiasm immediately turned to a tenacity that was all too familiar. Princess Noel Giraudeau de Montacroix was both the most appealing and frustrating woman he'd ever known.

"I told you," she said, "we're in this together."

"And if I said I didn't want you with me?"

"I'd say that's too bad. Because I have no intention of letting you leave without me."

"Has anyone ever told you that such mule-headed behavior is most unfeminine?"

"Why don't you ask me if I care?" She shook her head. "Besides, you have to take me with you. Unless you want me to be hung for murder on the same gallows the good people of Whiskey River built for you."

Despite the seriousness of their situation, Wolfe laughed. "You do not fight fair, Princess. However, you make a good point. I suppose I have no choice in allowing you to accompany me to Silverton."

Having gotten her way, Noel was diplomatic enough not to argue. "Thank you."

He laughed again, a rough, resigned laugh and shook his head. "Go get your things," he said. "I've arranged for Many Horses to bring you some of his younger brother's clothing to wear on the trip."

"It'll be much easier riding in trousers," Noel said gratefully. Although Second Mother had given her some herbal cream to rub on her chafed thighs, she wasn't looking forward to getting back in the saddle again wearing a skirt.

"That was my thought. But pack your red dress to wear when we arrive in Silverton. With that hair and your white complexion, there's no way we can pass you off as Dineh."

"So you'd rather I look like a prostitute?"

"Next time you steal clothing, I'd suggest taking something more subdued," he suggested.

"If there had been a more appropriate outfit for escaping a posse, I certainly would have selected it."

"If you'd have stayed in your room the way any sensible woman would have under the circumstances, you wouldn't be forced to escape a posse," he told her dryly. "We'll be leaving camp in thirty minutes. There is something I must do first."

Before she could answer, he turned and rode away.

After changing into the trousers Many Horses gave her, gathering up her belongings and saying goodbye to Second Mother, Noel grew impatient. Rather than wait for Wolfe to come fetch her, she went looking for him.

She found him down at the spring, sitting on a rock beside the water, spinning tales of Navajo gods and of the hero twins who'd first fought the giant, to a rapt audience of children seated in a semicircle at his feet.

That he relished his role of storyteller was more than a little obvious. It was when she found it so easy to imagine him telling similar stories to his own children—*their* children—that she realized she'd fallen in love with Wolfe.

As she waited for him to finish the tale, Noel's mind reverberated with that amazing thought. And although she could not understand a word, the emotion in his tone held her as spellbound as the children.

When the story ended, the children loudly begged him to tell another, but he shook his head, then told them something that had them all looking at Noel. As he stood up and walked toward her, a dozen pair of dark eyes followed him.

"They remind me of my sister and me," Noel said with a smile. "Always asking for one more bedtime story before *Maman* turned off the light."

"Someone needs to keep the stories alive," he said, somewhat defensively, Noel thought.

"Of course that's important," she said. "And no one tells them better than you."

"Ah, but you are undoubtedly prejudiced."

All the love she was feeling for him shone in her eyes as she smiled up at him. "Of course I am." She wanted to touch him, only a hand to his cheek, but restrained herself, worried that such an outward sign of emotion would embarrass him in front of the children who were watching them with unblinking attention.

"But that doesn't change the fact that you're a wonderful storyteller, Wolfe. Which is why people will still be reading your stories a hundred years from now."

The idea, which should have pleased Wolfe, did not. Because it reminded him that at any moment his princess could return to her own world. Her own time.

Would he remember her? he wondered, knowing that he would.

Would she remember him? That was only one of the questions that were gnawing at Wolfe's gut as they rode out of the Canyon de Chelly camp.

NOEL WAS NOT particularly disturbed when Wolfe did not speak during the long ride out of the canyon and across the high desert. Having grown accustomed to his thoughtful silences, she knew that no amount of prompting, pleading or threatening would coax a solitary word from his lips. He would talk when he was ready, and not before.

While Noel was drinking in the magnificent scenery that was so unlike her homeland, Wolfe remained deep in thought. He was thinking about the events that had nearly led to his death. About that damn book— *Rogues Across Time*—she alleged to have brought with her from the future that described his death by hanging.

And, as they rode side by side across the vast open, lonely land, he thought about the chances, slim as they were, that Bret Starr could actually clear his name.

He also, of course, thought about his princess. And her claim of having crossed time to come to Whiskey River in the first place. He wondered if she'd be surprised to learn that he did not consider the idea as outlandish as a white man might. There were, after all, more things on earth and in the heavens that any one man could possibly understand.

Such knowledge usually led to a type of serenity in the face of the astounding. One that was rooted not in submission, but in acceptance. There had been a time when ancient man were terrified by an eclipse. And although Wolfe now knew the scientific cause for the seeming disappearance of the sun or moon, the sight nevertheless strummed innumerable primal chords deep within him.

Those instinctive, primitive feelings had been born in the very first man and continued throughout succeeding generations. The same could be said about the need of a man for a mate.

Which led him back, full circle, to the princess Noel.

Wolfe sighed inwardly, as his troubled thoughts went round and round, like a leaf caught in a swirling whirlpool.

After they'd been on the trail about five hours, he decided it would be safe to stop. If he'd been alone, he would have kept going, but observing the shadows beneath her eyes and taking into consideration her recent lack of sleep, Wolfe decided that if she didn't get some rest soon, she'd end up falling off her horse.

He led them off the trail, to the base of a rugged red mountain, into a grove of cottonwood trees.

"We'll stop here."

Watching him dismount with a lithe yet powerful grace, Noel experienced a familiar fluttering in her heart. A fluttering that grew even more intense as he lifted her to the ground.

When their eyes met, she thought—hoped—that he might kiss her again. But instead, he released her and walked off to hobble their horses in a grassy spot, allowing them to graze.

While he took care of the horses, she knelt beside the river, and cupping her hands, scooped up some fresh cool water.

Watching her drink from the crystal river, Wolfe thought what a lovely picture she made, how natural she looked in this remote and wild place that he loved so deeply, when he saw something that made his heart leap to his throat. A mountain lion, crouched on the limb of a tree directly over her bent head.

"Don't move," he said in a low rough voice.

"What—"

"And don't say a word. Just stay right where you are." Wolfe feared that if he told her the danger she was in, she'd move suddenly, or scream, causing the giant cat to make its move. Better that she just follow his instructions. Explanations could come later. After she was safe.

The warning in his gruff tone—echoed in his flinty eyes—was enough to make Noel shut her mouth so fast and so hard her teeth slammed painfully together. Her heart trebled its beat and she grew instantly chilled, as if a thunderhead had suddenly moved across the sun.

"You must trust me."

Her eyes—wide and terrified—nevertheless assured him that she did. With her life.

"Whatever I do, whatever happens," he said softly, "don't move. I don't want to risk hurting you."

She swallowed and managed a slight nod, watching as he slowly took the winchester from the saddle.

"I'm going to pull the trigger on three. The minute I do, I want you to move as quickly as you can to the right . . . One."

The tension surrounding them was palpable. "Two," he said softly as he watched the giant cat get ready to spring.

Inside, Noel was screaming. Outside, she pressed her lips together and held her breath.

Just when she didn't think she could remain silent another moment, Wolfe said, "Three!"

Then, with a movement too swift for her to follow, he lifted the rifle and pulled the trigger. At the same time, Noel rolled away from the tree, nearly landing in the river.

The shot rang out, the sound ricocheting against the red rocks. A moment later, she heard a mighty roar, followed by the breaking of tree limbs as the mountain lion came crashing down.

It was then she screamed.

He was dead. Looking down at the lifeless cat, Wolfe felt the cooling waves of relief wash over him. Relief that was tempered with a faint sadness. It was a beautiful animal. Brave and strong and born to hunt, like the Dineh warrior of old. Wolfe knew it bore them no personal animosity. It was only following its nature.

Even as he knew he'd had no choice, it did not escape Wolfe's notice that the same guns that had conquered the Dineh had allowed him to conquer another of nature's own.

Although time seemed to have slowed to a crawl, all those thoughts raced through his mind in an instantaneous flash. The following second, he was kneeling beside Noel and dragging her limp body against his, holding her tightly, as if he would never let her go.

"It is all right," he told her, over and over again. She felt like ice in his arms and her trembling reminded him of the golden leaves of the white-barked aspen quaking in the autumn breeze. He pressed his lips against the top of her head. "You are all right."

She was clinging to him, as if to keep from falling off the edge of the earth. He could feel her heart pounding with a wild out-of-control beat.

She risked a sideways glance at the dead mountain lion, then shut her eyes tight and shuddered as she thought how close she'd come to dying this day. "You saved my life."

"As you saved mine," he reminded her. "If you had not shot Black Jack to keep him from killing me, neither of us would have been in this place at this time."

"If you hadn't stopped to help me after my accident, we wouldn't have been in the Road to Ruin when Black Jack arrived."

"And if you hadn't bought that book, telling you about my alleged crimes, you would have remained in your own time." His hands roamed up and down her back, in an attempt to soothe, rather than excite.

And Wolfe would have hanged. Which, Noel reminded herself, could still happen. When that thought proved too painful to contemplate, she twined her arms around him, holding him even tighter.

As her quaking thighs pressed against his, and he felt the softness of her breasts yielding to the superior strength of his chest, Wolfe found his mutinous body becoming more and more aroused.

"You are very brave, Princess Noel de Montacroix."

The admiration in his deep voice should not have meant so much to her. But it did. Looking up at him, she lifted a hand to his dark cheek and managed a smile that only wobbled slightly.

"So are you."

"I am Navajo. I have no choice. But white people have a choice. No one would care if you were not brave."

"I would care."

Her remarkable sky-blue eyes were sober. He smiled. "Yes."

She was like no other woman he'd ever met. Like no other woman he would ever meet. When he thought of how close he'd come to losing her, his blood ran as cold as Whiskey River in January.

Wolfe looked down into her exquisite face, watching as the soft pink color slowly returned to her cheeks.

Then, unable to resist that gilt-edged feminine invitation in her eyes, he lowered his mouth to hers.

As she had the other times he'd kissed her, Noel opened for him readily. Willingly. The completeness of her surrender had desire boiling up inside him, burning him alive from the inside out. One hand fisted in her pale hair, tilting her head back. The other hand settled at the small of her back, pressing her into his heat.

Never in his life had Wolfe wanted a woman more than he wanted this one at this moment. He wanted to devour her, to conquer her, to brand her, claim her for his own. He wanted to feel her hot and wild and naked, bucking beneath him, matching him thrust for thrust, as they rode together into oblivion.

His body was strong and rock-hard. His hands were big and rough. And wonderful. His mouth was like fire on her's, sending flames flicking through her veins.

Tangled emotions—need, hunger, pleasure, love— all rushed into her so swiftly her head spun. When his lips scorched a path up the side of her face, desperate for more, she moaned a shuddering protest and dragged his mouth back to hers.

He could have kissed her endlessly. From her forehead, to her toes. And everywhere in between. But as he caught her hand and lifted her fingers to his mouth, he saw the soot and remembered how he'd spent the night.

"I need a bath," he said, forcing the words through deep drafts of breath.

What Noel needed was Wolfe. Here. Now.

"Later." She framed his blackened face with her hands, seeing past the burnt ash to the man beneath. This man who, against all that was logical, was her destiny. This man she loved.

His fingers curled around her wrists and he pulled her hands from his face, scowling at the black stains. Not only had he been on the brink of taking her like some savage, he realized he looked like one, as well.

Although Many Horses had told him that he should wear the ashes for three days, to ensure all the evils were extracted from his body, once again caught between two worlds, Wolfe felt uncomfortable being with her, like this.

"There's a spring just down there," he said, jerking his head in the direction of a narrow trail weaving through the thick brush. "It flows into a pool. I won't be long."

To Noel's amazement, he released her. Then, behaving as if nothing had happened, he stood and began to walk away.

"Wait a minute!" she called out to his strong straight back.

"What is it now?"

Wolfe shot an impatient look over his shoulder. He was angry. Not at her, never at her, but at himself.

He wanted her. At the same time, he didn't want to hurt her. And, even if he did survive, there was nothing that he, as an outlaw, could ever offer a princess.

Except his heart.

Wolfe cursed inwardly. He felt as if he were trapped between two great stones. If either one moved, or if he moved, he'd be ground to fine powder. Just like the corn grown by the Dineh in Canyon de Chelly.

There was no future for them. That much, Wolfe knew. And if she wasn't sensible enough to guard her warm and generous heart, he would have to protect it for her.

"I don't understand." She dragged her hands through her hair, spreading dark soot through the shimmering silver strands. "That kiss—"

"Should not have happened," he said brusquely. "You are an engaged woman," he reminded her. "I have no right to kiss you. No right to want you. So, if you will only cooperate by not being so damnably seductive, perhaps we can get through this without making any more careless mistakes."

That said, he turned away again and disappeared into the trees.

Stunned into silence, Noel stood there, hands on her hips, staring after him.

"A mistake?" she muttered. "A *careless* mistake? How dare he call something so perfect a *mistake?*"

Once again, the temper she'd not been aware of before coming to Arizona Territory, flared. Pausing only long enough to take off her engagement ring, she headed after him.

10

MISGIVINGS TUGGED at Wolfe's conscience like minnows worrying a piece of bait. He was floating on his back, watching the pewter clouds building up on the horizon, when he heard her stomping down the path.

So, she was angry. He wasn't surprised, given the way he'd treated her.

As much as Wolfe hated the idea of upsetting Noel, in his mind it would have been far worse to have given in to temptation, to have done what they both wanted, to have made love to her until they were exhausted, then leave her. Or lose her.

Both of which were, of course, inevitable.

Against all reason, he had reluctantly come to believe her incredible tale of having traveled across not only continents, but time, in a noble attempt to save his life. Yet, even if she did succeed in her goal, once her mission was completed, what would keep her from returning to her own time? Alone. The thought of her leaving was like being stabbed with a thousand knives.

And if she failed, if he *was* hanged, as that chapter in her damn book related, then he would be the one leaving her. Alone.

There was no way this could work out, Wolfe had decided. So why make things worse?

"You're wrong, you know."

Her voice was soft but firm. He turned his head and saw her standing on the bank, her hands on her hips, her chin jutting out in that stubborn way that made him want to kiss her again.

"About what?"

"About making things worse. How could love make anything worse?"

After she'd entered his vision during the Blackening Way, he was not surprised by her seeming ability to read his mind. "Nothing can come of it."

"Perhaps not." Her eyes, and her tone, were grave. "But it's not a unilateral decision. I believe I should have a vote."

"This is 1896," he said. "Women have not won suffrage."

A ghost of a smile played at the corners of her mouth. That luscious mouth he could still taste. That sweet mouth he longed to taste again. "Ah, but I'm a woman ahead of the time."

Wolfe thought it said something about her spirit that she could find something humorous in their situation. And then, as she began to undress, he forgot to think at all.

"I love you, Wolfe Longwalker." Her fingers opened the first silver button on her blouse, giving him a tantalizing glimpse of creamy flesh. "Which doesn't make much sense, I suppose, since you haven't exactly welcomed me into your life."

Another button followed. Then another. As he watched and waited, Wolfe's mouth went uncharacteristically dry.

"However, since this is a difficult time for you," she said as she worked her way down to the waist, "I'm willing to overlook your occasionally curt behavior."

She shrugged out of the velveteen blouse, revealing perfect breasts barely covered in that skimpy piece of

French lingerie. The sight of her nipples pushing against that flowered silk, sent heat rushing through his groin, turning him hard as a rock.

The sight of his arousal, which he didn't even bother to try to conceal as he continued floating on the azure water, sent hot fingers of need through Noel. Although she felt as if every nerve ending in her body had suddenly turned raw, she, a quiet, reserved woman who'd never attempted to seduce a man in her life, continued her impromptu striptease.

"What I will not agree to," she continued calmly, even as her knees were shaking, "is allowing your misguided sense of morality to keep us from experiencing whatever pleasure we can steal. Whenever and wherever we can steal it."

She kicked off the suede boots Second Mother had given her. Then, after unlacing Many Horses's brother's trousers, she stepped out of them.

Wolfe had been in some of the finest whorehouses in this country and in Europe. He'd bedded royalty. And beauties. But never had he seen a woman capable of affecting him the way Noel was at this moment.

The first time he'd witnessed that skimpy underwear, he'd been a man on the run searching out injuries on a woman who'd annoyingly sidetracked his escape. Now he was viewing her as a man viewing a woman he desired. And he found her perfect.

"Do all the women in your time wear such things?" he asked, his rough hoarse voice revealing masculine approval.

She unconsciously ran her fingers over her silk-clad breasts, experiencing a shock of sensual pleasure at the feel of her ultrasensitive nipples. "Quite a few women do."

He shook his head, as if unable to believe his good fortune. "None could look as desirable as you." He stood up in the waist-high water. "As enticing as I find that flowered silk, I want to see you without it. Then, I want you. Here. Now. In every way possible."

She saw the raw hot hunger in his eyes. Heard it in his voice. Infused with a sense of feminine power she'd never known, Noel granted him that same slow smile women had been using to seduce men since the beginning of time as she unfastened the front hook and shrugged out of the lace-trimmed bra.

Even from this distance, she could hear his sharp intake of breath as the bra joined the rest of her clothes on the ground. Then, she hooked her fingers in the low-riding waistband of her bikini panties and slid them with agonizing slowness over her hips and down her thighs.

The pale curls at the juncture of her long slender legs shimmered like moondust, making his palm itch with the need to touch.

"You are so incredibly beautiful you steal my breath away."

Having grown up in the shadow of her glamorous older sister, Noel had never felt incredibly beautiful. Pleasing, perhaps. Even pretty, in a good light on a good day. But beautiful?

Yet, as their eyes met, exchanging sensual messages too sweet to analyze, she felt like the most beautiful woman in the world. In both their worlds. Noel laughed out loud from the joy she was feeling.

"What I am is lonely," she complained prettily. Although flirting had definitely been Chantal's style, not her's, in this place, at this time, it seemed amazingly natural.

Her laughter was like music, wrapping around him, through him. "Then perhaps you should join me." He held out his hand and began walking toward her.

Wolfe Longwalker was the most magnificent man she'd ever seen. His bronzed body was as hard as this wild land his people had called home for so many centuries. He had the lean, sinewy strength of a warrior and his thighs were beautifully muscled from a lifetime of riding horses across the vast high plateau.

"You're the beautiful one." She'd never seen a more perfect male specimen, not even depicted in all those bronze and marble statues back home in her family's palace.

Wolfe's low, pleased chuckle proved that his hearing was as perfect as the rest of him. "It's a good thing the other men in my clan can't hear you say that."

"I don't care what the men in your clan might think. I only care about you. Besides, it's the truth." Drawn by the same power that had drawn her across a century, Noel began walking toward him.

She experienced a momentary shock at the first touch of the water against her heated flesh, then, as her body became accustomed to the temperature, she found herself becoming warmed even more by the heat in his mesmerizing indigo eyes.

"You are beautiful, Wolfe Longwalker. And I want you so very, very much."

His smile was a wicked slash of white in his dark face. "Far be it from me to deny a princess anything her royal heart desires."

They met about six feet from the red-stone bank. "This is your last chance," he warned, his eyes locked on hers. "If you don't tell me no right now, there will be no turning back."

Knowing that there'd been no turning back since Sabrina had passed on Chantal's invitation, Noel said, "Thank God."

He sighed his surrender. And then he touched her.

It was only a palm to her cheek, but it shook Noel all the way to the bone. His hand was dark and, like the rest of him, large, at least twice the size of hers; on the inside of his wrist was a birthmark in the shape of a wolf's head that the unknown author of *Rogues Across Time* had described. The mark that had earned him his name. Although his touch was tender, the raw strength was evident.

He murmured something in his native Navajo that needed no translation. Noel knew exactly what Wolfe was feeling because she was feeling it herself.

Wonder.

Love.

And, more to the point at this suspended moment, *need.* He took her hand in his, intending to lift it to his lips. It was then he realized that she'd taken off a great deal more than her clothing.

"Where is your promise ring?"

"In your saddlebag." The decision not to marry Bertran had not been made hastily. It also had nothing to do with her feelings for Wolfe, although falling in love with him had shown her exactly why it would be a mistake to wed a man she could never give her entire heart to. "I did not want anything—or anyone— to be between us when we finally made love."

The water was lapping at her breasts. Heat was pooling between her thighs. Her soft lips curved in a slow, seductive female smile as she twined her arms around Wolfe's strong neck. She tilted her head back and waited for his kiss.

She did not have to wait long. As if suffering from a lifetime of need, he groaned and claimed her mouth.

The kiss went on and on. The hands that dived into his jet hair were shaking and urgent. The lips savaging her's were hard and hungry.

He tore his mouth from hers, and devoured the milk-pale flesh of her breasts, first one, then the other, ravenously feasting like a man who'd been starving all his life.

Her body was a throbbing, pulsing mass of sensations. With his mouth and teeth, with his rough strong hands, he treated her to a dizzying pleasure just this side of pain. Burning with need, moaning his name, she dug her nails into his shoulders as she arched her back, inviting, demanding him to take more.

When his hand slipped between them, his fingers pulling those silvery curls before plunging deep inside her, Noel cried out.

It was reckless. Wild. It was savagery tempered with love. And it was love that made it wonderful.

"Please," she gasped. Beneath his mouth, her heart was pounding like a jackhammer. "I want you. Now." Her body clenched wildly at his clever, wicked fingers, even as it demanded more. "Oh, please, hurry."

His teeth closed around a nipple and tugged. Wolfe felt a corresponding tightening deep inside her that ripped at the last vestiges of his control like a grizzly's claws. "I want you ready for me."

"I am ready," she moaned, rotating her hips in instinctive feminine demand. "Can't you tell?" Her hands fretted down his back, below his waist, pressing him even tighter against her.

As urgent as she, he lifted her. "Wrap your legs around me, Princess," he growled in her ear as he cupped her bottom in his wide dark hands.

She willingly did as instructed, locking her legs around his hips, holding on to his shoulders. With his first thrust, a fireball exploded inside her, filling her with heat, touching her deep where no man had ever touched her before. Deep in her body. And her heart.

He'd felt the unexpected barrier too late, as he tore through it. Wolfe cursed. A low, guttural sound that came deep from his chest and sounded like a growl. But then he felt her surrounding him, warm and wet and welcoming and felt the explosions ripping through her, massaging his penis like a thousand hot stroking fingers. A red haze came over his mind.

Need curled tightly at the base of his spine as he tightened his hold on her and began to thrust—deeper, harder. Once, twice, a third time, and then, shouting out her name, which echoed around the crimson red rocks, he poured himself into her.

Wolfe had no idea how he managed to get them both back onto dry land. But somehow, they were lying beside each other on his bedroll beside the water. Her cheek was on his chest, his hands tangling in the silken strands of her hair.

"How did my bedroll get down here?"

"I brought it with me."

"I didn't see you."

She ran her hand down his chest, loving the feel of his hard muscles beneath her fingertips. "You were pretending not to notice me."

He lifted her hand to his lips and kissed her fingers, one at a time. "I always notice you. Even when I don't want to."

He eyed her gravely over their linked hands. "Why didn't you tell me you'd never been with a man?"

Noel sighed. She'd feared this was going to prove a problem. She lifted her head and sighed again when she viewed the dark and guarded expression that was so like the one he'd worn when she'd first tried to get him to admit who he was back at the Road to Ruin.

"I thought men preferred virgins. Especially in these times."

"Some men do. I've never been one of them."

As much as she loved him, that stung. "I'm sorry I was such a disappointment."

Wolfe cursed, wondering how he could make things any worse. "Don't be foolish." He cupped her chin in his fingers and lifted her gaze to his. Her crystal-blue eyes were moist and shiny, making him feel even more the bastard. "You were anything but a disappointment, Princess. In fact, if you'd been any hotter, you would have set the water to boiling."

She smiled through the threat of tears. "It was you. No man has ever made me feel like that."

He picked up her hand and ran his fingers across the place that had so recently worn that sparkling diamond. "Not even your fiancé?"

"Bertran is a very wonderful man," she hedged. It was bad enough that she'd just betrayed the man she'd promised to marry. She could not demean him, as well.

"I didn't ask that." His eyes were locked on her's, looking hard. Looking deep.

"If Bertran had made me burn, you would not have made love to a virgin just now."

The flash of rebellious loyalty in her gaze made Wolfe feel guiltier than ever. "I'm sorry." He turned her hand over and pressed a kiss against the inside of her wrist, rewarded when he felt her pulse jump. "I should not feel so good about your broken engagement. But I have to admit that the idea of you returning home to another man's bed—"

"Never." She quickly pressed the fingers of her free hand against his mouth. "I love you, Wolfe Long-walker. Only you. There will never be another man for me."

When a very strong part of him wanted that to be true, Wolfe decided that he was one rotten son of a bitch. Who was he, after taking her with such force and haste, to demand that she live a life of celibacy? Just because he hated the idea of any man ever touching her. Tasting her. Lying with her like this.

"Neither of us knows how long this will last—"

"I do," she cut him off again. "Forever. A lifetime."

"Forever," Wolfe repeated, loving her unwavering determination. Loving *her*. "Since we've already determined that time is relative, are we talking your life-time? Or mine?"

"Either. Both," she said without hesitation. "Although I've inherited Katia's gift, I don't possess the power to see my own future. I have no idea what's going to happen in the next few days. I also don't know if I'm destined to stay here, or return to my own time.

"But," she said, turning their hands so she could see the wolf's head at his wrist, "the one thing I *do* know is that I will love you through all eternity." She pressed her lips against the birthmark. "Whatever the future holds."

Wolfe had learned to use the white man's words well. He earned a very good living with them, they'd been his gateway to a world not many individuals, let alone Dineh, would ever experience. But never had Wolfe ever heard words that affected him so deeply. "I will love you, too, Princess Noel Giraudeau de Montacroix," he pledged. "For all eternity."

He traced her lips with a fingertip. "If I had known you were inexperienced," he murmured as he brushed his lips against hers, "I'd have taken more time." He stroked her cooled flesh from her breast to her thigh. "I wouldn't have taken you like some wild animal."

His caressing touch was warming her, rekindling flames, stoking fires. "Actually," she said on a breathless laugh as his roughened fingertip brushed across a nipple, "I rather enjoyed that part."

"So did I." He stroked the taut nub with his tongue, enjoying her soft, rippling sigh of pleasure. "But there are other ways."

She was melting. Like a candle beneath the bright golden sun. "You'll have to show me."

His lips curved against her creamy flesh. "With pleasure."

He drew her into his arms and as the shadows grew longer, Wolfe showed Noel exactly how much he loved her. All afternoon long.

Noel had never been happier. Which was foolish, she realized, since she'd never been in a more precarious situation. The trip across the Arizona high desert and into the Rocky Mountains was long and difficult. Not wanting to tire out the horses, they did not ride as hard and as long as they had on the way to Canyon de Chelly.

As anxious as she was to get this matter settled, Noel knew that the trip to Silverton would always be the most wonderful time of her life.

They talked freely, sharing stories of their lives, their dreams. When he spoke of his youth, those long lonely months spent so far away from his beloved Dinetah and his clan, she felt like crying.

Although Wolfe did not want to risk using his rifle because the thunderous crack could draw attention to them, they did not want for food. The river teemed with fish, the land with small animals. Once, after he'd heard the warble of a wild turkey, Noel watched in awe and admiration as, with a single underhand toss of his knife, Wolfe provided them with that night's dinner.

It was a night made for lovers. With no man-made lights to diminish the effect and no haze of industrial pollution, the starlight was dazzling.

"I've never seen so many stars," she murmured as they sat beside a campfire, eating the savory roast turkey. "Not even in the Montacroix planetarium."

He laughed, enjoying her pleasure. And her awe. "There is a legend that First Man and First Woman made the stars to serve as lights on those nights when the Old Man Moon was too tired to make his journey across the sky.

"They planned an orderly arrangement, but Coyote tricked them by scattering them across the sky and they've been that way ever since."

"You portrayed Coyote as a troublemaker," she said, thinking back on Wolfe's book of stories.

"Among other things."

"Still," she decided, "I'm glad he scattered the stars." Wolfe smiled. "So am I."

"May I ask a question?"

They'd shared so much, been so open with each other, the hesitation in her tone puzzled him. "Of course."

"It's about your father." Noel watched Wolfe's face close. But when he did not immediately cut her off, she continued across the conversational minefield. "Do you ever wonder about him?"

"No."

Well, that was certainly short and sweet. Noel took a deep breath and tried again. "But half of who you are, what you are, comes from him, so—"

"I don't *ever* think about him," Wolfe said curtly, cutting her off with a vicious swipe of his hand. "When I was younger, I thought about him all the time. I thought about castrating him so he could never do to any other woman what he did to my mother. I thought about slicing his throat. I thought about staking him out in the summer sun. I thought about innumerable ways of torturing him, each more excruciating than the last.

"Finally, Second Mother and Many Horses convinced me that all I was doing was hurting myself. So, I put the bastard away in a box, deep in my mind, and I never, ever opened it again."

"But what if there were extenuating circumstances?"

The look he gave her was as hard as flint. As cold as sleet. "There are no extenuating circumstances for rape."

"What if it wasn't rape? What if they loved each other?"

"He was a *bilaganna*. She was Dineh."

"I'm white. And you are Dineh," she argued softly.

"What we have is different," he insisted. His features were drawn taut beneath the bright red headband. "But even if that were the case, which it was not, leaving a woman with a child in her belly to die along some murderous trek is inexcusable."

"As wrong as that was, it was government policy," Noel said carefully. "Your father was not responsible."

"Planting a seed in a woman does not make a man a father. He was responsible for her death. If she'd been stronger, if she hadn't been carrying me, she would not have died."

"And you would not have been born."

He shrugged. "I cannot see that the world would have missed my presence."

Her eyes misted as she framed his face between her palms. "*I* would have missed your presence." She pressed a tender kiss against his firmly set lips. "Can't you see how the hatred of your father has come to color your life?"

"Should I forgive those soldiers who drove my people from their ancestral lands? Should I forgive them for all the Dineh who died during those years? Should I forgive those who make warriors stand in line like slaves for bug-ridden flour and rotten meat? Should I forgive my father for my mother's death?"

"You are not the only man to lose family," Noel told him gently.

"No. But I may be the only man who doesn't forget. As much as I love you, I cannot change who—and what—I am. I cannot trust the *bilaganna*."

"You can trust me."

Gradually, as her lips continued to pluck tantalizingly at his, Wolfe succumbed to temptation.

He drew her down onto his bedroll and, putting aside the unpalatable discussion, made long sweet love to her.

As THEY CLIMBED high into Colorado's San Juan Mountains, growing emotionally closer with each mile, Wolfe and Noel were almost able to forget their dangerous situation. Noel knew that whatever happened after she'd cleared his name—she could not allow herself to think that she'd fail in this all-important mission to save Wolfe—she would always consider these long and uncomfortable days the happiest of her life. Because they'd been spent with the man she loved.

But even in this halcyon time, a shadow lurked on the horizon, one they tried desperately to ignore.

From their mountaintop vantage point, Silverton looked like a child's miniature village, the kind that usually had a toy train running through it. Riding the switchback trail down the mountain into the mining town, Noel felt a very strong sense of foreboding.

As she rode beside Wolfe down Blair Street, music from the dance halls drifted on the night air, mingling with the sound of laughter and the occasional sound of breaking furniture as fistfights broke out.

Wolfe pulled up at the back of The Irish Rose.

"Bret Starr's in here." Noel's voice trembled with excitement as she felt the hair at the back of her neck stand up. "I can feel him."

Her voice was not the only thing trembling. As he lifted her down from the back of the horse, Wolfe could feel the anticipation coursing through her veins.

"It is not enough simply to find the artist," he reminded her.

"I know." She kept her hands on his shoulders. "But if he was there when that cabin burned, and those people died—"

"There's still no reason to believe he'll be willing to come back to Whiskey River with us to testify for me. Or that anyone will believe him if he does."

"Don't worry." She went up on her toes and pressed her lips against his. "Everything's going to work out. I can feel it in my bones."

Despite his continued misgivings, Wolfe found it impossible to resist the hope shining in her wide blue gaze. He ran his hands up her back, rewarded when she began to tremble in a way that had nothing to do with her anticipation of meeting Bret Starr but everything to do with her love for him.

"And such exquisite bones they are," he said against her mouth.

The kiss was long and sweet and ended too soon for either of them.

The woman who opened the door was at least twenty years younger than Belle. And about fifty pounds lighter.

"I'd heard you escaped," she said, taking his hand and drawing him into the kitchen. Unlike the kitchen of the Road to Ruin, which had been lighted by gaslight, The Irish Rose was electrified, revealing the wealth to be made in this remote mining town. "But the word is that you've gone to Mexico."

"I thought of it. But something changed my mind."

His words drew her attention to Noel, who was still standing right inside the doorway. "I also heard about what you did," she said with a friendly smile. "That was some shooting. There's already a song about the lady in red who shot Black Jack. It's quite the rage."

"That's all I need," Noel said dryly. "They can play it at my hanging."

"Oh, no one's looking for you," the madam said quickly. "In the first place, Black Jack didn't die, more's the pity—"

"He didn't?" A cooling rush of relief flooded over Noel.

"No. Belle dressed his wound and although she tried to keep him at the Road to Ruin, to give you two plenty of time to make your getaway, he left the next morning in search of both of you. He came in on the train yesterday, as a matter of fact. I heard he's gone on to Ouray.

"I'm Rose." She held out a slender beringed hand to Noel. "But my friends call me Rosie."

"And I'm Noel."

"Nice accent. Is it real?"

"Yes."

The madam skimmed a quick, professional glance over Noel. "You're a little road-rumpled, honey. But a soak in a hot tub and a change of clothes will take care of that. So, how'd you like to work here?"

"She's not a whore," Wolfe said quickly.

Rose's shrewd eyes narrowed at his harsh tone. "I see."

Not wanting to waste time on lengthy explanations, Noel decided it was time to be direct. "We're here looking for a man—"

"Got plenty of those upstairs," Rose agreed easily.

"This man's an artist. Bret Starr?"

"Got him, too."

Noel shot Wolfe an I-told-you-so look. "May we talk with him?"

"Well, now, I suppose you can talk all you want. But Bret isn't going to be much use to you. He spent last night drowning in a bottle of whiskey, muttering about fires and Indians and lies."

"So he *was* there!" She grabbed Wolfe's arm. "We really need to talk with him. He can prove Wolfe's innocence."

"Much as I'd love to help with that, honey, the man wouldn't remember his own name right now. You'll have better luck if you allow him to sleep off all that whiskey."

"We don't have time for that!" Noel insisted.

"We've found him," Wolfe said. "He's not going anywhere. A few more hours isn't going to make that much difference. Especially if the posse thinks we're headed toward Mexico."

"It's dangerous," she insisted, knowing that waiting would be a mistake. "What if Black Jack returns from Ouray? What if he didn't really go there in the first place? What if the men who killed those settlers know about Bret Starr? What if we've walked into a trap?"

"You'll be safe here," Rose assured them. "I'll have my men stationed at both doors. And the bottom of the stairs."

"It's best we stay here," Wolfe said quietly. The same thoughts had all occurred to him during the ride from Canyon de Chelly. But it wasn't as if they had a great many choices.

"But the book," she reminded him. "Today's the day you're supposedly captured."

"What book?" Rose asked.

"It's nothing." Wolfe's smile belied his own concerns. He hadn't forgotten that chapter in *Rogues Across Time*. He just hadn't wanted to dwell on it. "Just a plot I'm working on for my new book."

He ran the back of his hand down the side of Noel's face in a gesture meant to reassure. "You weren't in the original story, either," he reminded her gently. "We're simply changing things. Everything will be all right."

Noel only wished she could believe that. But having come to know Wolfe well during these days together, she knew the futility of arguing.

"If you're sure—"

"I'm sure." He bent his head and brushed his lips against hers in a light kiss that promised more to come. "I'll take the horses to the livery, while you get settled in our room."

He handed her the saddlebags, then give her another kiss—a longer, deeper one that took her breath away. And then he was gone.

"I have a terrible feeling about this," Noel fretted.

"He'll be fine," Rose assured her. "In the meantime, why don't you pretty up for your fella? I'll have a maid bring some bathwater up to Wolfe's usual room and—"

"Wolfe has his own room?" Although she'd accepted the idea that Wolfe had not exactly lived the life of a monk before meeting her, this thought was admittedly disturbing.

"Well, hell, honey," the madam said, looking at Noel with surprise, "he *is* a man. With a man's needs, if you get my drift."

Noel murmured something vague that could have been an agreement. Or a curse.

"But, although Wolfe's no saint, most of the time he used the room for writing. He wrote *First Man, First Woman* here," she said.

"You're the Colorado Rose." Noel had wondered about that dedication.

"That's me." Rose grinned. "And before you start pulling hair, I promise you, honey, I have *never* slept with Wolfe. Oh, not that I haven't been tempted," she admitted as she led Noel up some back stairs. "But since I kinda like my heart in one piece, I have a rule against getting involved with men I could fall in love with."

"And Wolfe falls into that category?" Noel asked.

Rose shot her a knowing look over her shoulder. "I think you know the answer to that, honey."

Although Noel didn't answer, she knew that her unruly love was written across her face.

"He'll be all right," Rose said gently.

"He has to be," Noel said fervently.

Now, if only she could make herself believe Rose's reassuring words.

WOLFE WAS LEAVING the livery when he sensed something or someone behind him. His hand dropped to his holster, but before he could retrieve his Colt .45, he felt the barrel of a rifle against his spine.

"Don't move, Longwalker," the familiar voice growled. "Or I'll blow you to kingdom come."

11

SOMETHING WAS TERRIBLY, horribly wrong.

Noel, who'd been pacing the floor of the room, rushed to the window just in time to see the group of armed men riding out of town. In the middle of the men she saw Wolfe, looking as grim as she'd ever seen him. Behind him rode Black Jack. And a man wearing the badge of a territorial marshal.

She flew out of the room and back down the stairs and was headed out the kitchen door, when Rose caught her by the arm.

"Where do you think you're going?"

"They've got Wolfe!"

"Aw, hell." Rosie shook her head. "That's a damn shame, honey. But you still haven't answered my question."

"I have to go help him."

"You may be a sure shot with that itty-bitty derringer of yours at three feet. But you want to tell me just how you intend to face down a posse?"

"I don't know, maybe I can cause a distraction, and allow him to get away—"

"Get shot in the back, you mean," Rose corrected. "You still don't get it, do you? Wolfe's an Indian. Most of those men would just as soon shoot him as look at him. You give them any excuse to do that, and you're signing his death warrant."

"You may have a point," Noel agreed reluctantly. "But I have to do something!" she said in a very uncharacteristic wail.

Rose cursed again. "Let's go wake up Sleeping Beauty," she suggested. "If we pour enough hot coffee down him, maybe he can help. Meanwhile, I'll send a boy to the jail to find out what that posse intends to do with Wolfe."

At first glance, Bret Starr certainly did not look like the answer to Noel's problems. His eyes, when she shook him awake, were as red-veined as a road map, his complexion, beneath at least a ten-day stubble, was the color of ashes, and she doubted that he'd bathed in the past month.

Reminding herself that he was her only hope, she began pouring Rose's robust coffee down him as she told her story.

"You saw the massacre, didn't you?"

"Didn't say that." His hands shook as he slowly, gingerly lifted the cup to his lips.

"It won't do you any good to lie. I know you were there. And I know you were so upset by what you witnessed, you ran away and came here and got drunk."

"Hell, honey," he said on something that was half laugh, half cough, "I'd have gotten drunk, anyway. That's what I do. Paint and drink. And lose at cards," he added on an afterthought.

"You paint what you see. And what you saw the day that cabin was burned was not Wolfe Longwalker."

"Of course it t'weren't. Why the hell would Wolfe want to kill settlers?"

"Some say because they're settling on land that used to belong to the Navajo."

"Some are wrong. Wolfe might not like what happened to his people, but there's no way he could kill an innocent family. Especially the kids."

"Wolfe likes kids, all right," Rose agreed, painfully reminding Noel of how she'd imagined him telling his stories to their own children some day.

"Who did you see that day?"

He didn't answer immediately, instead taking another long drink of coffee. When he drained his cup, Rose leaned forward and immediately refilled it.

While he blew on the coffee to cool it, a young boy wearing overalls without a shirt came barreling into the room. "I heard the sheriff say the marshal was takin' Wolfe back to Arizona Territory on the afternoon train," he announced. "To hang him."

No! She simply was not going to let that happen. Determined to change the ending of Wolfe's chapter in *Rogues Across Time*, Noel turned back to Starr.

"You have to tell me what you saw that day."

"Why don't you quit yappin' at me and think who else might not want those settlers on the land?" he retorted grumpily.

"That's what all this is about?" Noel asked. "Land?"

"Hell, lady, everything out here is about land. Grazing rights, mineral rights, water. The person who controls those things is the man who's going to survive."

She thought about what she'd read of the West, thought about the farmers who'd moved west in their covered wagons, seeking a new life while bringing with them everything the current residents hated—civilization, cities, temperance and... The answer came crashing down on her: barbed wire fences.

"It was ranchers, wasn't it?"

"Might've been," he hedged.

"You have to come back to Whiskey River with me," she insisted. "Right now."

"How about when hell freezes over?"

"But Wolfe's going to be hanged if you don't go back and testify."

"That'd be too bad," he allowed. "But from my view, it'd be a lot worse if I ended up shot in the back. Which is what could happen if I risk going up against ranchers."

"He's got a point, honey," Rose said. "Any man who can kill a sleeping child wouldn't hesitate to shoot a drunk no-name artist."

The madam's words, which caused Starr to bristle, gave Noel an idea. Having spent a great deal of time with Chantal's artist friends, Noel knew that while they might pretend to turn up their noses at wealth, the one thing they all lusted after was fame.

In a last-ditch attempt to convince him, she pulled the invitation out of her bag. "Look at this," she said, sticking it under his nose. "It's yours, isn't it?"

He squinted as he studied the drawing. "How the hell did you get this?"

"That's not the point. It's your work, isn't it? Done right after the massacre."

"It's mine."

"This is an invitation," she said, knowing that he and Rose were going to think she was crazy, but having no other choice. "For an art gallery showing in Washington, D.C."

"My work is going to be shown in the nation's capital?"

It was the first real sign of interest she'd witnessed. Noel had known he'd like that idea. "Yes. In 1996."

"What?" He stared at her as if she'd just grown a second head. "You're crazy."

"No. I'm not." She pulled one of Wolfe's books out of the bag and held it out to Rose. "You said Wolfe wrote this while he was staying here."

The madam's expression was not all that different from Starr's. "That's right." She frowned as she took the paperback and skimmed through the pages. "But I've never seen a book like this one."

"I know. Look at the copyright page."

"The what?"

"On the inside. At the beginning."

Rose opened the book to the page in question. "I'll be damned," she said, shooting a startled look at Noel. "It says published in 1996."

"That's right. I brought it with me."

"From the future?" While Rose looked decidedly skeptical, Starr, on the other hand, was suddenly sitting forward, as if more than a little interested in the idea.

"Exactly. I can't explain how I did it, I'm not sure about that, myself. But it did happen, and I know I'm here to clear Wolfe's name, and this invitation is the key. Which means that Mr. Starr is my only chance."

"Even if what you say is true, it's still too damn dangerous," he complained. He studied the invitation again. "I kinda hope you aren't loco. Because I like the idea of my work still bein' around in 1996."

"Did you notice the theme of the show?"

His rheumy red eyes skimmed the page. "Western artists."

"*Unknown* western artists," Noel told him.

His weathered face drew into a scowl as that idea sank in.

"Of course," Noel went on to suggest, "if you returned with me to Whiskey River and told the truth, you'd become famous."

"Famous and dead."

"But your art would live on."

She could see him mulling that one over. "I'd need some money to get away. Go to Mexico, perhaps until things calmed down." He rubbed his stubbled chin at the idea. "They say the women there are all hot-blooded."

"That's what I hear, too," Rose said, exchanging a hopeful look with Noel. "And it's so warm, they hardly wear any clothes."

"I could sure as hell get used to that in a hurry."

"Margaritas by the sea isn't such a bad way to hide out," Noel said.

"Margaritas?"

"It's a drink. Made with tequila and lime juice."

"I like tequila, all right. Don't know about the lime juice." He fell silent again, running his hand around the gilt edge of the invitation. "Famous, huh?"

"Famous," Noel and Rose said in unison.

With a silent apology to Bertran, Noel took her engagement ring out of her pocket. She'd retrieved it from the saddlebag earlier, in case the artist might need additional incentive to help.

"This should pay for a great deal of tequila."

He held up the ring to the electric bulb. The diamond captured the light, splitting it into rainbows. "You know how they define an opportunist?" he asked what Noel took to be a rhetorical question. "A man who, when he finds himself in hot water, decides to take a bath." He pushed himself off the bed. "Let's get going."

Noel's sigh of relief was audible. "When does the train leave?"

Rose glanced at the gold watch pinned to the bodice of her dress. "You've got an hour."

"That'll allow us time to get Mr. Starr cleaned up. And get him a new suit so he'll look presentable in court."

"That's going to be a problem," Rose said. "It's Sunday. There's not a mercantile open anywhere in the state today."

It was Noel's turn to curse. "All right," she said, "we'll just have to do what we can."

Forty-five minutes later, a freshly bathed Noel was studying the artist, who, while now also bathed and cleanly shaven, was still in desperate need of a change of clothing. As was she. Unfortunately, Rose's girls were not even as well turned out as Belle's, which made her red dress the best possible choice.

Frown lines etched their way between her eyebrows as she considered how they'd look—a whore and a drunk—showing up in court to proclaim Wolfe's innocence. Deciding to face that bridge when she jumped off it, Noel said goodbye to Rose, accepted a loan for the tickets, then dragged the hungover artist to the station just as the train to Arizona was boarding.

Although he didn't see her, Noel saw Wolfe, bound and shackled, surrounded by some very grim-faced men. The fact that they were taking him back to Whiskey River, instead of shooting him here, gave her renewed hope.

Glaring back at the leering ticket taker, she purchased tickets for herself and Starr.

As much as she longed to be with Wolfe at this trying time, she knew that it would be safer to take another car. Deciding it would be best not to be seen with Starr, either, she instructed him to board first.

She waited a few minutes. The train whistle blew, announcing the imparting departure.

"Bo-oarrd!" called out the conductor.

She'd just started to board, when a deep voice behind her made her jump. "What do you think you're doing?"

She spun around, one hand diving into the pocket of her skirt, her fingers curving around the grip of the derringer. It was the conductor, who was glaring at her in a decidedly unwelcoming manner.

"Boarding the train," she answered, hoping her anxiety didn't show in her voice or expression.

"Not my train."

Rose had assured her they weren't looking for her. However, Rose could have been wrong, Noel reminded herself. "I don't understand."

"It's simple. This is a respectable train. Not some immigrant special. No animals."

She followed his glare down to the yellow dog, who was sitting beside her, head tilted, ears pricked, as if following the conversation. Damn. Noel's mind whirled as she tried to come up with a solution. The dog had stayed loyally by her side since that terrible night he'd helped her confront Black Jack. She was not about to abandon him now.

"He won't be any trouble—"

"No mangy mutts."

"He's not mangy." Indeed, Rose's boy had bathed him in the leftover soapy water, leaving him smelling a bit like lilacs. And wet dog.

"No dogs."

"Perhaps he could ride in the baggage compartment?" Noel suggested, seeking a compromise.

"I said, no dogs. Now, if you want to stay here with the mutt, fine. Otherwise, you'd better get on board."

The dog whimpered, looking from Noel to the gruff man and back to Noel again. "But—"

"Excuse me." A smooth voice interjected its way into the argument.

"Yes?" she said.

"I couldn't help overhearing your dilemma. Perhaps I can provide a solution."

"Oh?"

"I hope you won't think I'm being too forward." The man tipped his hat as his gaze took a long tour of her body, so attractively showcased in the low-cut red dress. "But I couldn't help noticing that you're traveling alone."

The way he was looking at her, undressing her with his eyes, made Noel want to slay him with a few well-chosen words. But, on second thought, as she took in his well-cut suit, she suddenly had a marvelous idea.

"Why, yes, I am," she said in a melodious, honied voice.

"Ah." He nodded. "Are you visiting from France?"

"You have a very good ear, *monsieur*." She granted him a slow, sexy smile designed to bring the average man to his knees. She'd seen Chantal use such a smile to her advantage numerous times during their teenage days. "Actually, my home is in Montacroix. In Europe."

"I know where it is." He returned his smile with one of his own, but she noticed that his eyes seemed to be plastered to her chest. "I'm a representative of the Manhattan Knickerbocker Trust Bank," he revealed.

"I had dealings with Prince Leon last year. It's a lovely country. At the time, I remember thinking the most beautiful women in the world must have all congregated in that one small Alpine nation."

"Flatterer." She fluttered her lashes and found herself wishing she had a fan to use as a flirting prop.

"It's the truth. However—" he brushed the back of a finger across his mustache "—if I'd seen you, all those other women would have definitely paled by comparison."

"Gracious, I can't remember the last time I received such a lovely compliment," she murmured coyly. "So, what is your solution, *monsieur?*"

"I'd like to invite you and your pet, of course, to share my private car."

"You have a private car? How delightful." She bestowed another of Chantal's man-killing smiles on him.

"It makes travel more convenient," he agreed, puffing out his chest with pride. "In addition to allowing you to keep your canine companion with you, you would be a great deal more comfortable," he said. "I guarantee the food will be better. Also, I have a very fine selection of French wine."

"Oh?" Ignoring the repeated whistle blast, she said, "Do you have champagne? I do so adore French champagne."

"Several bottles from the finest vineyards," he assured her.

"Well, that is enticing." She chewed thoughtfully on a fingernail. "And it would surely be more relaxing. Could I take off my shoes? They do *so* pinch."

"Sweet lady, you could take off anything you please."

"Well." She took a deep breath that threatened to have her breasts popping out of the dress entirely. "I believe I'd quite enjoy sharing your car with you, Mr. . . ."

"Knickerbocker." Satisfaction mingled with lust gleamed in his eyes. "Jeremy Knickerbocker."

"You own the bank?" She managed to appear suitably impressed.

"My father is president. My great-great-grandfather established it. On land once owned by Indians."

"There seems to be a lot of that going around these days," Noel muttered.

"Excuse me? I didn't quite hear you."

"I'm sorry." Another winsome smile. "I said that I was quite impressed." Noel put her hand on his arm. "Please, Mr. Knickerbocker, lead the way."

Noel had grown up surrounded by beautiful, priceless things. She'd traveled the world in first-class accommodations. But even accustomed to luxury as she was, she was impressed with the splendor of Jeremy Knickerbocker's private railroad car. The walls were polished mahogany, crystal chandeliers sparkled, brass fixtures gleamed. The chairs were covered in a lushly soft velvet the color of the bordeaux from the Montacroix vineyards. Matching velvet curtains with gold tassel trim framed windows covered in snowy lace panels.

"Gracious," she murmured, her surprise not feigned. Even the famed Orient Express was not this extravagantly decorated.

"As I promised," he said, "it's quite comfortable."

She looked up at him through her fringe of lashes. "You must be a very important man."

"Some people might say so. However, even important men get lonely. Especially when their work entails so much traveling." Outside the private Pullman car, the whistle blew one last time, signaling the train's departure from the station.

Inside, the dog walked over to a sunbeam that was streaming onto the Oriental rug through the car window and settled down with a deep, satisfied groan.

When the banker ran a finger up her arm, it was all Noel could do not to shudder. "I certainly understand how it feels to be lonely." That treacherous finger was now trailing its way across her shoulder. "Did you say something about champagne?" she asked brightly.

Irritation flashed in his eyes, but he reined it in, reminding himself, Noel concluded, that it was a long way to Arizona.

"Make yourself at home," he suggested, waving a hand toward the red sofa. "I'll get us some refreshments."

The champagne was as excellent as he'd promised, as smooth as she would have suspected, given the luxurious appointments surrounding her. She sipped it slowly, smiled often, giving him enticing, stolen glimpses of her breasts, her calf, the delicate arch of her foot, clad in the black stockings Rose had given her. And all the while, she continued to refill his glass. Again and again.

Conversation flowed as easily as the wine. Fortunately, Jeremy Knickerbocker did not lack for subject matter. He found himself fascinating, and certain that she would also, proceeded to tell her everything about himself, his illustrious family, the famous people he met traveling the world in his dealings for the bank.

"Are you married?" She idly dipped a finger into the sparkling gold wine, watching his eyes glaze over slightly as she put the finger between her lips.

He frowned and tugged at the ends of his brocade vest. "Well, actually, I do have a wife back in New York," he revealed reluctantly. "However, there's a problem."

"She doesn't understand you," Noel guessed.

His frown deepened. "I'm afraid not. She also doesn't care about the . . . uh—" he pulled at his bow tie "—the more physical aspects of matrimony."

Noel ran her fingers up and down the stem of her glass in a flirtatiously subtle caress that did not escape his attention. She watched as little beads of moisture formed on the skin above his mustache.

"I've heard that's the case with some women." She shook her head. "Although I've never quite understood their feelings, I do feel sorry for them."

She turned, tucking her stocking feet beneath her voluminous skirt. As she leaned toward him, the crimson satin gaped open, giving him a weakening glimpse of her breasts, all the way to her waist. "May I speak frankly, Mr. Knickerbocker?"

"Of course, my dear." The words came out on a croak. She watched his Adam's apple bob as he swallowed. "And the name is Jeremy."

"Jeremy." She drew it out, lingering lovingly over it, caressing it with the silken French tones of her native language. She put her hand on his chest and felt the rapid beat of his heart. "I don't want you to think me too forward."

"Never," he said quickly. He covered her hand with his.

"I want you to understand my circumstances." She played with the folds of her skirt with her free hand. "What I am—what I appear to be—well, I wasn't always this way."

"I find you delightful, just the way you are." He ran his free hand down the silken slide of her hair.

"Thank you. But you see, I'm afraid the rigid rules of society—even in Europe—do not favor a female who enjoys the physical expression of affection between a man and a woman."

Her eyes were as limpid as a cocker spaniel's as she gazed up at him. "Because I crave such affection, I'm afraid that I'm viewed with disfavor in the eyes of many of my peers."

"Only by jealous, coldhearted females who envy your feminine appeal," he assured her quickly in a voice that was now practically choked with masculine needs. "Believe me, my dear, the men of this world thank God every day for creating such delightful women as you. In fact, although I realize it's a bit premature in our relationship to be admitting to such a thing, I believe I may be in love with you."

"Why, aren't you the sweetest thing?"

She'd no sooner gotten the words out than he lunged, pushing her onto her back and crushing his open mouth against hers in a wet sloppy kiss. When he stuck his tongue down her throat, she gagged; when he took their joined hands, pressing her palm against the tumescent sex beneath his trousers, all the time trying to delve beneath her voluminous skirts with the other, Noel realized that she was on the brink of getting in over her head.

"Please, Jeremy!" She dragged her mouth from his and struggled to sit up. "My dress! You're crushing it."

"I'll buy you a new dress." His fingers were squeezing her thigh above her stocking with a force she knew would leave bruises. His tongue created a wet swathe across her breast. "A dozen new dresses." He was bucking against her. "A hundred."

"Please," she repeated, pushing against his surprisingly hard shoulders. "It's a very long trip. Shouldn't we at least be comfortable? Wouldn't this be far more satisfactory if we didn't have so many clothes on?"

Her suggestion had the desired effect. With a low groan, he retrieved his hand from beneath her skirts and sat up.

"You are," he said, heaving heavily from exertion and hunger, "a very remarkable woman."

"I like to think so." Noel reached out and began to unbutton his waistcoat.

"What are you doing?"

"Undressing you, of course."

"I thought you'd go first."

"Well, we could do that," she agreed silkily. "Then you could do all the work afterward. Or—" she ran her fingernail up his leg and felt him jerk "—I could show you how a woman from Montacroix, with hot French blood flowing in her veins, makes love to a man she finds devastatingly appealing."

Bingo! She watched the possibilities flicker in his champagne-glazed eyes.

"I'm yours." He held out his arms. "Have your wicked way with me, my dear."

"Oh, Jeremy." She ran her fingernail around his mouth. "That's precisely what I intend to do."

With hands that trembled from excitement, rather than sexual desire, Noel slowly stripped him of his jacket, his vest and his shirt. His chest was covered with a thick dark mat of fur so different from Wolfe's sleek hard body.

"I do so want you," he groaned as he grabbed at her breasts. "I want you. Now."

"Not yet." Tamping down yet another surge of revulsion, she evaded his touch. "Anticipation is half the fun. And I promise you, Jeremy, the wait will be well worthwhile."

She knelt on the Persian rug and dispensed with his shoes. Then she began unfastening his pants. When her palm brushed against his erection, he closed his eyes and moaned.

She stripped the trousers off him. His eyes were still closed, his head lolling against the back of the sofa.

"Are you going to take my underwear off, too?" he asked hopefully.

"I'm sorry, Jeremy."

The change in her tone, from sultry to matter-of-fact, managed to filter its way into his alcohol-sodden brain. He opened his eyes, blinking rapidly as he viewed her standing over him, pointing the derringer at the most vulnerable part of his anatomy. The part that was rapidly shrinking.

"What are you doing?"

"I'm afraid I'm robbing you."

"If it's money—"

"No. I don't want any money, Jeremy. I just want your suit."

12

"MY SUIT?"

"I need it for a friend," she explained, continuing to hold the weapon on him as she tugged the gold braided rope down from the draperies. "Please, hold out your hands."

"You're going to tie me up?"

"I don't have any choice." She sounded honestly reluctant. "But if you do exactly what I say, I promise you won't be harmed in any way."

Fear coalesced into anger. "You bitch."

"Now, Jeremy," Noel said silkily, "is that any way to talk to the woman you professed to love?"

She tied his wrists and ankles, considered stuffing one of the damask napkins into his mouth, but afraid he might suffocate, decided against it.

When the train stopped in Durango for a meal break and to take on water, Noel reluctantly gagged her prisoner, left the car, told the conductor that Mr. Knickerbocker was sleeping and had asked not to be disturbed. Then she located Bret Starr who was standing in line, waiting for his meal to be served by one of the fresh and lovely Harvey girls who worked the train stops in the West.

"Don't ask any questions," she said quietly. "Just come with me."

"I'm hungry," he complained.

"I have plenty of food. Better than this," she said, glancing around at the simple fare. "I've also got you a new suit."

"Say no more." Handing his tray to the boy behind him, the artist followed her out of the trackside Harvey House dining room.

The banker's suit fit as if it had been tailor-made for Starr. Looking the artist over, Noel nodded her satisfaction. "You look like a wealthy substantial member of the community. I only wish I had something else to put on."

"I think you look real pretty in that," Bret assured her.

Noel laughed. "What is it about men that they get all hot and bothered over a red dress?"

"I think it's nature," Bret said.

"Or idiocy," Jeremy Knickerbocker, who'd had the gag taken out of his mouth again, muttered.

Amazingly, they managed to get along reasonably well, during the twelve-hour trip to Arizona, considering the circumstances. With her usual flair for calming troubled waters, Noel managed to convince the banker, who she'd allowed to don a velvet dressing gown, that he was taking part in a grand adventure that would provide entertainment for at least a decade's worth of dinner parties.

And although he was obviously disappointed that he was not going to be able to bed the sexy lady in red, he did accept, with some display of pleasure, the pen-and-ink sketch made of him by Bret Starr.

"You should take care of that," Noel advised. "Mr. Starr is going to be very famous. It will provide a legacy for future generations of Knickerbockers."

As Jeremy Knickerbocker put away the drawing for safekeeping, the whistle sounded, announcing their arrival at the Flagstaff station.

"Well, as much as I've enjoyed your hospitality, Jeremy," Noel said with a friendly smile, "I'm afraid it's time to say *adieu*." She stood up and shook out her skirts.

"We're getting off here?" Starr asked, obviously surprised.

"*I'm* getting off. You and Mr. Knickerbocker are continuing on. According to the schedule, there's a Phelps Dodge payroll train scheduled to leave Flagstaff for Whiskey River in an hour. I intend to be on it."

"What about Longwalker?"

"I'm counting on you to keep them from hanging him until I get there."

"That's easier said than done," he muttered.

Noel knew his negative attitude was partly due to her refusal to allow him any alcohol during the long trip.

"Belle O'Roarke will help you. Hopefully, I'll be arriving with the cavalry an hour behind you."

"Ain't no cavalry in Flagstaff," he muttered.

"That's what you think." She went over to the liquor cabinet, retrieved from her pocket the key she'd taken from Knickerbocker earlier and opened it, taking out a bottle of cognac, which she put into a carpetbag lying nearby. "If you carry out your part of the mission, Mr. Starr," she said, "this bonus will be waiting for you.

"I am sorry, Jeremy." Her expression revealed honest regret. "I hate to continue to steal from you, however—"

"I know," he grumbled. "This will provide a decade's worth of dinner-party stories."

"That's the spirit." A genuine smile bloomed on her face and in her eyes. Leaning down, she kissed his cheek. "Thank you for everything. And, just a word of advice? You may want to try seducing your wife the next time you are in New York."

"My wife? Why would I want to do that?"

"Most women enjoy it. She might, as well. Which would, in turn, provide you with a bit of that female companionship you say you're lacking. It's merely an opinion, but there is a theory that there are no frigid women. Just inept lovers."

With that, she left the car, the dog, as usual, on her heels.

ALTHOUGH NOEL left the dog outside the redbrick building housing Judge Daniel Cavanaugh's office, her own appearance earned overt disapproval from the secretary seated behind the wide oak desk.

"I'd like to speak with the judge," she said.

"Do you have an appointment?" His tone suggested that he knew a woman such as her would not.

"No."

"Well, then—"

"I know Judge Cavanaugh would want to see me."

His pale brown eyes behind the round steel-framed glasses flicked over her dismissively. "I doubt that."

She reached into her pocket and took out the envelope Second Mother had given her. "Please give him this." Her calmly insistent tone was that of a woman accustomed to getting her way.

Plucking the envelope from her fingers, holding it gingerly, as if it were contaminated, he left the outer office.

Noel began to count. She'd barely made it to ten, when the door to the private office burst open and a tall man with a shock of silver hair emerged.

"Who are you?" he demanded. His indigo eyes locked onto hers. "And how did you get this?"

She glanced over his shoulder at the obviously curious young man. "I will explain everything. But I think you might prefer having this conversation in private."

Muttering something that could have been an agreement, he waved her into his office. As she walked past the secretary, it was all Noel could do not to shoot him a victorious look.

"All right," the judge said without preamble, gesturing her to a chair on the visitors' side of the desk. "What's this all about? If you have it in mind to blackmail me because I was once in love with a beautiful—"

"I have no intention of blackmailing anyone," Noel said. She may have shot a man. And made another undress at gunpoint, then held him hostage and stolen his brandy, but she could not imagine lowering herself to such shoddy behavior. "Did you?"

"Did I what?"

"Did you love her?"

Those eyes turned to flint in a way that so resembled Wolfe's eyes when he was angry that Noel had no doubt this man truly was Wolfe's father. "I don't see where my youthful feelings are any of your business."

"That's where you're wrong. Because I'm in love with your son."

He waved away her declaration with an impatient hand. "I don't have a son."

"Yes. You do. And he's currently in Whiskey River. About to be hanged for a murder he didn't commit."

She took a deep breath. "You may have heard of him. Wolfe Longwalker?"

Shock waves moved across his face. "That can't be."

"It's true." She stood up, leaned across the table and took hold of his hand. "He has this same mark." She'd noticed it when he'd gestured. "He was born on the Navajo's Long Walk. Unfortunately, his mother died after giving birth to him. It was her sister who gave me your letter.

"I need you to return with me to Whiskey River to save your son's life. There's a train we can take leaving the station in forty-five minutes."

He rose to his feet without a moment's hesitation. "Let's go. You can fill me in on the details on the way."

It was raining when they arrived in Whiskey River. An icy rain fell unceasingly from a darkened sky and thunder boomed from anvil-shaped gunmetal-gray clouds. The dirt road leading through the town had turned to mud.

As she hurried down the wooden sidewalk from the station, past the scaffold that was smoldering from recently being set ablaze—by Belle and Bret, she would learn later—Noel's heart was pounding in her ears. Surely she wasn't too late!

And then she saw him.

Just as he'd appeared in her vision, Wolfe sat rigidly astride his blood-bay mare, his hands tied behind his back. He was clad in buckskin trousers and a pair of boots. His long jet hair was held back from his forehead with a red cotton headband. Rain ran in rivulets down a rigidly muscled chest the hue of burnished Arizona copper but which Noel knew from experience was ever so much warmer.

His dark blue eyes—his father's eyes—were directed out across the fierce red landscape as Jess Buchanan, the territorial marshal, looped the thick, braided horse-hide rope around Wolfe's neck.

"You must stop these proceedings immediately," Daniel Cavanaugh shouted.

Buchanan turned toward the newcomers. "'Afternoon, Your Honor," he said. "Come here to watch a murderer get his just rewards, have you?"

"I've come here to ensure justice is done."

"Well, now, Your Honor, sir, I hate to quibble with you, but this Injun has already been tried and convicted. Would've hanged, too, if he hadn't escaped."

"You're fortunate he did," Wolfe's father said. "Since it saved you having to explain to St. Peter why you hanged an innocent man."

A loud murmur went through the gathered crowd.

Beneath his handlebar mustache, Buchanan's mouth drew into a harsh scowl. "He's been found guilty."

"In a trial that was a joke. A trial conveniently conducted by a circuit judge known for his propensity to take payoffs." The anger in Cavanaugh's tone was as sharp as a whip. "Any crime dealing with the native population requires a federal judge," he reminded the marshal. "And that happens to be me."

"You were outta town," the marshal mumbled.

"I was in Washington. But I'm back now. So we can move these proceedings to the courthouse."

The mumbles increased, but knowing when he was outranked, the marshal reluctantly removed the noose from around Wolfe's neck.

"What are you doing here?" Wolfe demanded when they came face-to-face on the courthouse steps. He was furious at Noel for having put herself at risk.

"Trying to save your stubborn neck," she retorted. "And by the way, I've brought your father along to help."

Every muscle in Wolfe's face clenched. He glared at the tall handsome man standing beside Noel. "I have no father."

Noel practically bit her tongue in half to keep from screaming at him. "Wolfe," she said, struggling for the patience that had once been her hallmark, "this animosity between our races has to end somewhere. Why not here? And now? With your father?"

"I told you—"

She pressed her fingers against his taut lips, forestalling his argument. "You once said you would do anything for me."

"It was the truth."

"Then talk to him, Wolfe. That's all I ask. Please."

The two men exchanged a look. Then Wolfe shrugged and returned his gaze to Noel. "I am only doing this for you."

Hope fluttered its hummingbird wings in her heart. "I know."

The conversation, held in private, did not take long. Wolfe's dark expression as the two men came out of the back room, was less than encouraging.

Noel's nerves were on edge as she sat in the courtroom, listening to Bret Starr's testimony. Relieved that he'd managed to stay sober, she felt that any reasonable person would find the story believable. Especially since he had no reason to lie. Well, she admitted, some modern courts might quibble that the four-carat diamond ring in his vest pocket might prove an incentive, but knowing that she was only paying him to tell the truth, she decided to overlook that nitpicky little point.

The new jury looked interested, she felt. But not quite convinced. Obviously, more than one had the feeling that Wolfe wouldn't be accused of the murders if he hadn't committed the crimes. And unfortunately, Wolfe had no alibi for the time of the massacre. And more distressing, he'd steadfastly refused to tell Noel where he'd been.

"Are there any more witnesses?" Judge Cavanaugh inquired, exchanging a glance with Noel that suggested he'd done his best.

Suddenly, a woman seated among the spectators stood up. "I'd like to testify," she said, her voice trembling with emotion.

"Do you have information relevant to this case?" the judge asked.

She took a deep breath and looked straight at Wolfe. "I was with the defendant at the time those settlers were murdered."

If that statement set off shock waves through the spectators, her next words had the effect of a dynamite blast blowing everything to kingdom come. "We were together at my ranch. While my husband and his friends set fire to that cabin."

After banging his gavel for at least five minutes, the judge managed to quiet the courtroom.

While the woman testified, Noel took the invitation out of her pocket. As she watched, the wording changed. The showing was now a retrospective of that famous western artist, Bret Starr.

They'd done it!

There would be no hanging here today!

"ALTHOUGH I AM SUPPOSED to be a writer, I do not have the words to thank you," Wolfe said.

It was several hours later and he and Noel had finally managed to slip away to Belle's private suite in the Road to Ruin. The yellow dog was downstairs, happily sampling scraps from the rack of lamb Belle had roasted to celebrate Wolfe's freedom.

"Then you're not angry? About your father?" She'd worried that although she'd saved his life, going behind his back, when he'd made his feelings so clear, might cost her Wolfe's love.

"I was, when he first introduced himself. But I understand all too well how it feels to be found guilty for something you did not do. And his explanation, along with that letter, proved he was telling the truth."

Wolfe frowned, thinking back on the startling revelation that had turned so much of what he'd always believed upside down. He and his father would never be able to make up for those years they'd missed. They may never be able to have a true father-son relationship. But he felt they'd taken the first steps to being friends today.

"How about you?" he asked. "Does it bother you to know that I was with another woman? A married woman?"

From the beginning, Noel had known Wolfe wasn't a saint. She also knew that he loved her now. "You've no idea how relieved I was. Why didn't you ever say you had a witness?"

"Mary was only a witness if she chose to testify. And she had her own reasons for not wanting to do that."

"Like a violent husband." Noel shook her head. "Some women made very poor choices."

"Strange words from a woman who fell in love with a convicted murderer from another time," Wolfe teased gently as he drew her into his arms.

She framed his handsome face in her hands. "I was afraid, once I saved you, that I'd be drawn back to my own time."

"I feared that, as well," he admitted. "However, since neither of us knows what the future holds, I suggest we stop wasting time by talking."

"Yes." She laughed with pleasure as he scooped her up in his arms and carried her into the adjoining bedroom. "Yes, yes, yes."

Basking in this stolen time that neither had expected, they undressed each other slowly, drawing out the moment with lingering kisses and caressing touches.

Wolfe lifted his head and glanced over at the bath Belle had instructed some unseen servant to prepare. "It seems our hostess has thought of everything."

"A woman of imagination, our Belle," she agreed, laughing as he lifted her again and lowered her into the warm water. She ran her hand over the curled edge of the hammered-copper slipper tub. Noel knew antique dealers who'd pay a fortune for this tub. Back home. When that thought reminded her that her time with Wolfe could be fleeting, she held out her hand. "Aren't you going to join me?"

The water rose as he settled in behind her, drawing her against him. "This reminds me of the first time I made love to you," he murmured against her neck as he took a bar of French milled soap and rubbed it between his hands, creating a froth of fragrant bubbles. "You were wet that day, too." He ran his soapy palms over her shoulders. "And warm."

"I was freezing when I first stepped into that pool."

"But not for long." He touched his lips to her neck.

"No," she said on a soft, rippling sigh, "not for long."

He spread the lather over her breasts. When his fingers skimmed over a nipple, she shivered. "Cold?" he asked.

"Actually, I think I'm burning up." Her head was spinning, filled with the fragrance of bath salts rising in a mist from the hot water, bedazzled by the touch of his hands on her body, the warmth of his breath against her neck.

"That's just the way I want you." He ran his hand up her leg, from her calf, to her knee, to the sensitive flesh of her inner thigh. "Hot." He pressed his hand against her. "Hungry."

"Wolfe, please—" She arched against his intimate touch, not caring that she was begging.

"Is this what you want?" He slipped his fingers into her slick moist heat, moving them in and out with a silky ease.

As delicious as his sensuous touches were, as clever as his hands could be, Noel needed more. Much, much more.

"I want you." She twisted in his arms, pressing her breasts against his slick wet chest as her avid mouth roamed over his face and her hands slipped between them, touching him as he'd touched her.

As many women as he'd known, as many as he'd bedded, it had never been this way for Wolfe. Every time was like the first time. He knew that if he were to make love to his princess every day for the next one hundred years, until they'd reached her time, he would never tire of the way she made him burn.

"Not yet." He caught her waist, stopping her as she began to lower herself down onto him.

"Wolfe—"

He ignored her faint protestation. "There are times, like now, when you seem like a dream," he said, standing up, drawing her to her feet, as well. The warm water sluiced off them. "And I'm terrified of waking up, because you might be gone."

"I know that dream." She pressed her hands against his chest, splaying her fingers against his coppery flesh. "Too well."

"I rather thought you might." He dipped his head and treated her to a kiss so tender, so sweet it brought tears to her eyes. "Whatever happens, I want you to know that you're my destiny, Noel Giraudeau. My life. My love. And somehow I will find a way to be with you. Forever."

Her lips began to tremble. Her eyes overflowed with tears. "Forever," she whispered.

He kissed the moisture from her cheeks and held her close for a long time as she wept silently, unable to bear the thought of losing him.

He spoke to her in his native tongue, the language of his heart, and although she couldn't understand the words, she knew that they were meant to comfort.

Much, much later, her tears stopped flowing, and although her breath still came in little hitches, her trembling had ceased, as well.

He pressed his lips against the top of her head.

"And now I want to make love to you in a real bed. With the lights on, so I can watch you as I take you over the edge. And so that I'll know, for certain, that you're not a dream, but a real flesh-and-blood woman."

She smiled through the filmy mist of tears. "How could any woman resist an offer like that?"

Never had Noel known such splendor. Outside the window, the night draped Whiskey River in a moonless cloak of black velvet. Inside, bathed in the flickering golden glow of the gaslight, Wolfe showed her ways of making love she'd never imagined, loved her in ways she knew she'd remember for the rest of her life.

At the same time, he encouraged her to spread her sexual wings, to touch him in places she'd never touched a man, to kiss him in new and exciting ways, to claim, to possess, until he was as seduced as she.

All thoughts of the future were burnt away by that same flame that ignited their bodies and hearts. They forgot the world—both their worlds—as they spent a long love-filled night designed to last a lifetime.

As he watched her sleep, Wolfe could feel her slipping away. Like illusive wisps of morning fog between his fingers. She was leaving him. As they'd both feared she would.

Not that she would ever be gone from his heart. Because Wolfe knew that whenever the wind blew through the trees, it would be Noel's voice whispering to him. When he looked at the sky, he knew it would be her face he would see in the clouds. And at night, he knew the tiny points of the stars brightening the black sky would be the twinkling of her magnificent eyes.

She would be everywhere.

And he knew, as he knew his own heavy heart, that someday, somehow, they would be together again.

IT WAS THE SUN streaming into the bedroom that woke her.

"Thank heavens," a familiar voice said with obvious relief. "You're awake."

"It seems so." Fighting against the cloud still settled over her mind, Noel forced her eyes open and found herself staring into a familiar face.

"Audrey?"

"It's me," the elderly woman agreed, strawberry curls bobbing as she nodded with enthusiasm. "I'll tell you, girl, you sure did give us a fright. When the sheriff found your car—"

"I had an accident."

"Skidded off the road into a ditch," Audrey agreed. "Sheriff Callahan saw the tire marks and figured you must have swerved for something. Maybe a deer?"

"Perhaps." Or a man on horseback. "I can't quite remember." She dragged her hand through her hair and glanced around the room, her gaze focusing on the wall calendar. The picture was of the towering rocks of Monument Valley, which she could remember with vivid clarity. "You didn't take me to the hospital?"

"We wanted to," Audrey assured her, "but the bridge over Whiskey River is out from all the flooding and the Medivac helicopter can't fly in this thunderstorm, so the doc examined you and said it'd be okay for you to stay here. He said you were just sleeping. Not unconscious, or anything, but I gotta tell you, honey, you've been zonked out for the past twelve hours and even though the doctor checked on you three times, and said you were okay, you sure seemed gone from this world to me."

Even as she fought against the threatening flood of tears, Noel felt her lips curving in a faint wry smile. "It felt that way to me, too." For someone who had been asleep for twelve hours, she felt horribly exhausted.

"I'll get you some tea," Audrey said. "And some soup and crackers. You've got to be hungry."

"I don't—"

"You need food," the robust innkeeper overrode her planned complaint. "No offense, honey, but you're too skinny, as it is. Men prefer a woman with a little meat on her bones."

"I'll keep that in mind," Noel murmured, remembering how Wolfe had found her perfect.

As she listened to Audrey going back downstairs, Noel leaned back against her pillow and closed her eyes. It had been real. She knew it. She was not like Dorothy, who'd only dreamed of Oz. Her adventure in Whiskey River had not been a product of a bump on the head. Her love affair with Wolfe had not been merely a sensual dream.

She glanced down at her bare left hand where she'd once worn a ring, and despite the fact that her heart felt as if it had been carved into little pieces, Noel found herself hoping that Bret Starr had enjoyed his life in Mexico.

Viewing the familiar *Rogues Across Time* on the bedside table, she picked it up, opening unerringly to the chapter on Wolfe Longwalker.

"Considered one of the West's most important writers," she read out loud, "after being falsely accused of murder, Wolfe Longwalker went on to live a full and productive life, still writing well into his eighties." Tears born of both sorrow and happiness filled her eyes. "He never married."

But he did, Noel knew.

They'd exchanged vows that last night together. Here in this very room.

Wolfe Longwalker would always be her husband. As she would be his wife.

Forever.

The following day, fortified with plenty of aspirin, Noel flew home to Montacroix. As soon as she landed at the airport, she went directly to the bank, where

Bertran served as vice president in charge of foreign investments.

"Noel." Her fiancé rose from behind his desk, surprise evident on his face. "I hadn't expected you back so soon."

"You hadn't expected me to leave in the first place," she said.

"True." He nodded. "Please, sit down. Would you care for some tea? Some mineral water?"

"No, nothing, thank you. I'm fine."

He studied her with concern. "You look pale."

"I suppose it's jet lag."

"You never get jet lag," he said, reminding her of one of the disadvantages of trying to be less than forthright with a man who'd known you all your life.

"You're right." She took a deep breath. "Bertran, we have to talk."

"I agree." He sat on the edge of his desk and began fiddling with his gold Waterman fountain pen.

"You do?"

"I recall saying much the same thing when I asked you not to leave for America."

"True, but I thought it was because the wedding—"

"That is what I wanted to talk about."

"Well." She looked at him, confused at the way this was going. All the way home, she'd rehearsed her speech so carefully, choosing her words so as not to hurt him. But no sooner had she entered his office than he'd thrown her off the track. "Would you like to go first? Since you've obviously been waiting longer? Or should I?"

"I believe the rule is ladies first," he told her.

"All right." Taking another deep breath that did little to calm the butterflies fluttering in her stomach, she went on to explain how, although she truly loved him dearly, and always would, she felt it would be unfair to both of them—and to whatever children they might have—if they went through with the planned wedding ceremony.

"As hard as I tried, Bertran, dear," she said quietly, her eyes earnest as they looked straight into his, "I could not love you in the way a woman should love a man she's promising to spend the rest of her life with."

Noel had not known exactly what to expect. She'd known Bertran would not display any temper. But would he be icily cold? Remote? Would he, heaven forbid, beg her to change her mind?

What she could not have guessed was that he'd laugh.

"Bertran?"

"Oh, Noel." He slid off the desk and took both her hands in his. "The reason I so wanted to talk to you before you left is because I was trying to find some way to say the same thing to you."

"You wanted to break off our engagement?" She stared up at him in disbelief. "Why?"

"For the same reason you just mentioned. All our lives, we knew we would marry. Such knowledge was safe. Predictable."

"Boring," Noel muttered.

"*Exactement*. There is something else." He ran his finger around his starched white collar, as if it had suddenly become too tight.

Comprehension dawned. "You've met a woman."

"An actress, actually. From America. New York. She arrived last month to appear in one of Sabrina's productions, and, well, she wanted to open an account, just while she was here, and one thing led to another and . . ."

He dragged his hand through his hair and cursed. A rich, earthy curse she'd never heard from him before. "Do you hate me too badly?"

"Hate you?" Noel laughed. "Darling, I could never hate you." She framed his distressed face between her palms and kissed him. A light, friendly kiss with no sexual overtones. "I told you, I'll always love you."

Two days later, Noel was in Washington, D.C., helping Chantal hang paintings for the gallery showing.

"So it's really over."

"Yes."

"Are we happy about that?" Chantal asked carefully.

"Very happy," Noel assured her.

"Good." Chantal's smile was as dazzling as ever. "So, what will you do now?"

Noel shrugged. "I'm not sure. At the moment, the only thing I do know is that I belong in Whiskey River." She took another framed drawing out of the carton. "There's an inn I might buy."

"You're thinking of running an inn?"

"Perhaps. Or perhaps I'll just live there."

"And do what?"

Noel shrugged. "Play it by ear, I suppose."

Chantal shook her head. "I think that's a very good idea. And very unlike you." Noel was infamous for her lists and schedules. "Are you certain you didn't suffer any head injuries in that accident?"

"I'm fine." She cut the string and began unwrapping the brown paper. "Truly."

"Well, I for one, think it's time you had a little enjoyment out of life. You've always worked too hard,"

Chantal said. She glanced over at the painting Noel was staring at.

"Oh, I like that one."

"So do I," Noel agreed as she studied the painting of a woman, clad in a red dress, holding a dapper, well-dressed man at gunpoint.

"Do you know," Chantal said thoughtfully, her gaze going from Noel to the painting and back to Noel again, "that woman looks a great deal like you."

Noel laughed, feeling happier and more carefree than she had in days.

Epilogue

NOEL HAD NEVER been happier. Three months after her return to Whiskey River, comfortably settled into her new home, she was in the front yard, weeding the garden, when the sound of a car engine coming up the long curving driveway caught her attention. Nearby, beneath an apple tree laden with fruit, her dog gave one quick sharp bark.

The big yellow dog had shown up her first day in the former bed and breakfast, behaving as if he belonged there. Which, she knew, he did.

"It's okay," she assured the animal. "I've been expecting company."

After spending the night dreaming of Wolfe, she'd awakened with a feeling of expectation. A feeling that had escalated when she'd reached into the drawer of the bedside table and discovered that the *Rogues Across Time* book had mysteriously disappeared. Fortunately, Wolfe's books remained on her bookshelf.

She stood up, experiencing a brief light-headedness and a faint fluttering in her stomach. Although morning sickness had kept her close to home, she did not resent the frequent nausea.

Because, along with Bret Starr's painting that Chantal had sent her—the one depicting her in the red dress, holding Jeremy Knickerbocker at gunpoint, the one currently hanging on her bedroom wall—this child growing in her womb was proof that her exciting, blissful time with Wolfe had not been a dream. Or a fantasy.

She may not have Wolfe, but she would have his child. Somehow, miraculously, proof of their love had transcended time and space.

As she watched, a man climbed out of a forest-green Jeep.

With a whelp of welcome, the dog went bounding over to him, dancing circles around his legs.

"Hello," he said, a friendly smile on his face as he approached her. With his right hand, he casually ruffled the dog's thick yellow fur. "I'm Mackenzie Reardon, owner of the *Rim Rock Record*."

"Oh, yes. Hello, Mr. Reardon. It's nice to finally meet you."

"It's a pleasure to meet you, too, Your Highness."

"Please." She took off her canvas gardening gloves and extended her hand. "It's Noel."

"Noel." As his hand closed around hers, a current surged through his fingers, into hers. Seeing the surprise in his eyes, she knew she was not the only one who'd felt it.

There was a long pause. A pregnant pause, Noel thought with inward humor.

"Well," he said, appearing reluctant to release her hand, "as I told you on the phone, it's not every day a European princess moves to Arizona's ranching country. I thought the paper's readers might like to know about your plans. And since you haven't felt up to coming to town—"

"I've been a bit under the weather. But I'm feeling much better."

"I'm glad to hear that." Friendly green eyes set in a tanned face swept over her face with what appeared to be genuine concern. "Nothing serious, I hope."

"No. Something quite wonderful, actually." She smiled. "I'm going to have a child."

Noel watched the questions in those emerald eyes, realized the truth was going to come out sooner or later and decided who better to spread the news than a newspaperman.

"My baby's father is dead," she revealed.

"I'm sorry." His eyes, which had drifted involuntarily to her still-flat stomach, returned to her's.

"Thank you."

A little pool of silence settled over them as she looked at him and he, in turn, studied her. Although his hair was a sun-streaked chestnut, rather than black, and his eyes were the color of emeralds, rather than a deep indigo, something about the newspaperman stirred a deep-seated recognition inside Noel.

Apparently, Mac was no less affected. He was looking at her. Looking hard, looking deep. "I'm sorry," he said finally, on a faintly embarrassed laugh. "I don't mean to stare, but I have the strangest feeling that we've met somewhere."

"I'm not as famous as my older brother or sister, but I've received my share of press. You've undoubtedly seen a photograph."

"I suppose that's it," he murmured absently.

Noel could see the lingering doubt in his eyes. A doubt that echoed in her own heart.

When he lifted his hand to drag it through his thick wavy hair again, Noel viewed the birthmark on his wrist. A mark that looked, remarkably, wonderfully, like the head of a wolf.

"Mr. Reardon, do you like lemonade?"

"Who doesn't? Especially on a hot day like this."

"How wonderful. And as it happens, I was feeling unusually domestic this morning and did some baking. Would you care to share a piece of chocolate cake with me?"

A dazzling smile wreathed his handsome face. "Princess, I'd be honored."

Infused with a warm, golden glow, Noel invited Mackenzie Reardon into her home.

*   *   *   *   *

If you've enjoyed reading about the residents of Whiskey River, Arizona, a place that JoAnn Ross says "is where anything can happen. And often does," then you won't want to miss her new Temptation miniseries
MEN OF WHISKEY RIVER. *In October, November and December 1996 enjoy three very magical romances featuring three sexy, unforgettable men and three beautiful and unusual women.*
Come and be spellbound!

Take 4 bestselling love stories FREE

Plus get a FREE surprise gift!

Special Limited-time Offer

Mail to Harlequin Reader Service®

3010 Walden Avenue
P.O. Box 1867
Buffalo, N.Y. 14269-1867

YES! Please send me 4 free Harlequin Temptation® novels and my free surprise gift. Then send me 4 brand-new novels every month, which I will receive before they appear in bookstores. Bill me at the low price of $2.66 each plus 25¢ delivery and applicable sales tax, if any.* That's the complete price and a savings of over 10% off the cover prices—quite a bargain! I understand that accepting the books and gift places me under no obligation ever to buy any books. I can always return a shipment and cancel at any time. Even if I never buy another book from Harlequin, the 4 free books and the surprise gift are mine to keep forever.

142 BPA AW6V

Name	(PLEASE PRINT)	
Address	Apt. No.	
City	State	Zip

This offer is limited to one order per household and not valid to present Harlequin Temptation® subscribers. *Terms and prices are subject to change without notice. Sales tax applicable in N.Y.

UTEMP-895

©1990 Harlequin Enterprises Limited

BRIDE'S BAY RESORT

UNLOCK THE DOOR TO GREAT ROMANCE AT BRIDE'S BAY RESORT

Join Harlequin's new across-the-lines series, set in an exclusive hotel on an island off the coast of South Carolina.

Seven of your favorite authors will bring you exciting stories about fascinating heroes and heroines discovering love at Bride's Bay Resort.

Look for these fabulous stories coming to a store near you beginning in January 1996.

Harlequin American Romance #613 in January
Matchmaking Baby by Cathy Gillen Thacker

Harlequin Presents #1794 in February
Indiscretions by Robyn Donald

Harlequin Intrigue #362 in March
Love and Lies by Dawn Stewardson

Harlequin Romance #3404 in April
Make Believe Engagement by Day Leclaire

Harlequin Temptation #588 in May
Stranger in the Night by Roseanne Williams

Harlequin Superromance #695 in June
Married to a Stranger by Connie Bennett

Harlequin Historicals #324 in July
Dulcie's Gift by Ruth Langan

Visit Bride's Bay Resort each month wherever Harlequin books are sold.

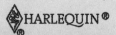

HARLEQUIN ®

BBAYG

The Wrong Bed? The Wrong Twin?
The Ultimate Temptation

It was ten years since Emily Rose had seen
"Chigger" Callister, but he'd grown up to be sheriff
of Bluster County and a magnificent specimen of
manhood, just as she'd pictured him in her bedtime
fantasies. She couldn't quite pin down his personality,
though. She never knew which Callister she was
going to see.

It was almost as if there were two of him.

Don't miss:

#591 TWIN BEDS
Regan Forest

Available in June wherever Harlequin books are sold.

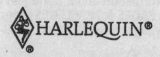

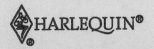